THIS COMIC BELONGS TO:

_____

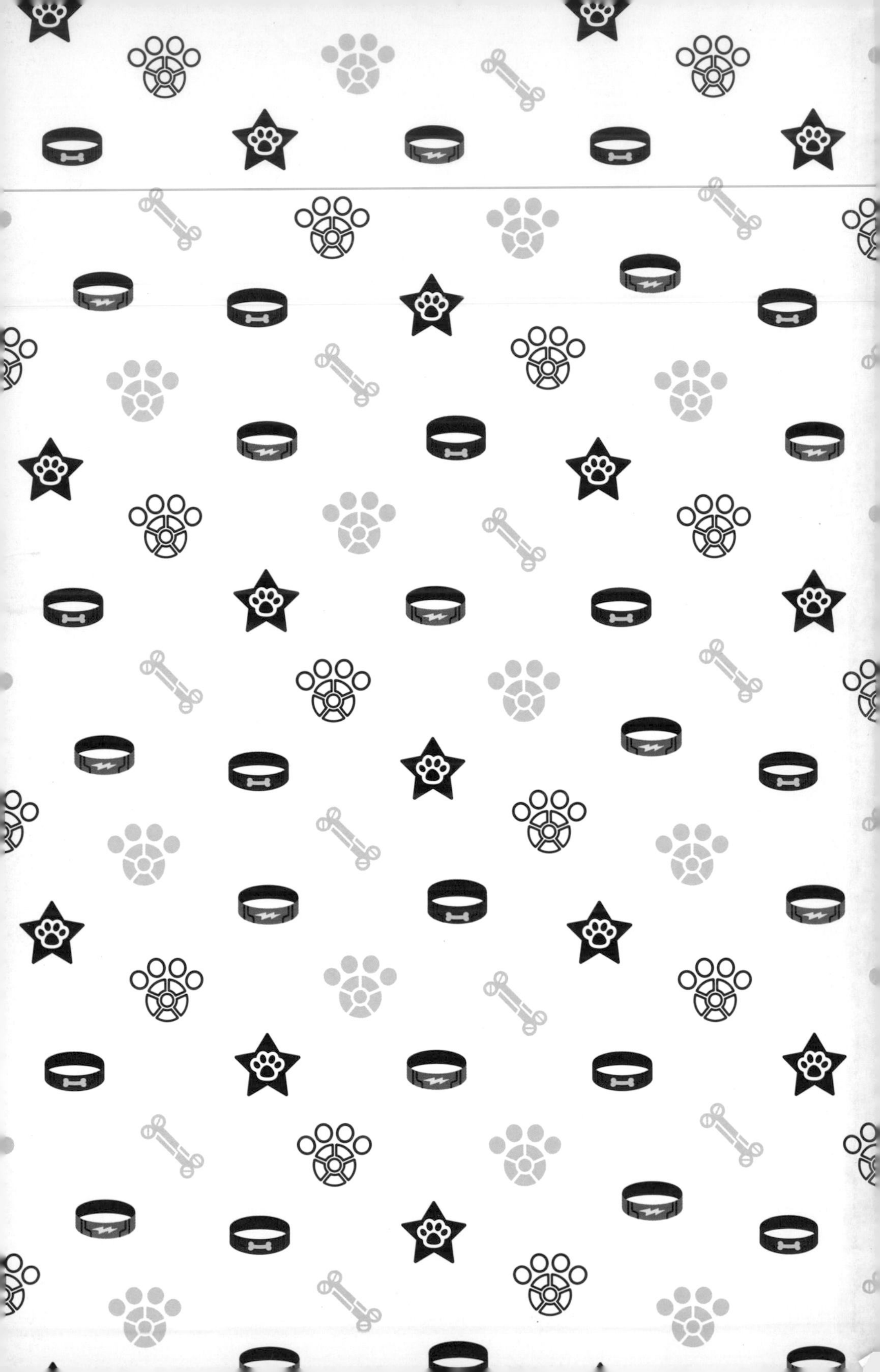

Disney

PUPPY DOG PALS

Published simultaneously in the United States and Canada by Joe Books Ltd,
489 College Street, Suite 203, Toronto, ON M6G 1A5.

www.joebooks.com

Hardcover and paperback published simultaneously: March 2018

Hardcover ISBN: 978-1-77275-674-6
Paperback ISBN: 978-1-77275-869-6
ebook ISBN: 978-1-77275-864-1

Library and Archives Canada Cataloguing in Publication
information is available upon request.

Printed and bound in Canada
1 3 5 7 9 10 8 6 4 2

Disney
PUPPY DOG PALS

THEIR ROYAL PUG-NESS

CINESTORY COMIC

JOE BOOKS LTD

MEET THE PUPPY DOG PALS AND THEIR FAMILY!

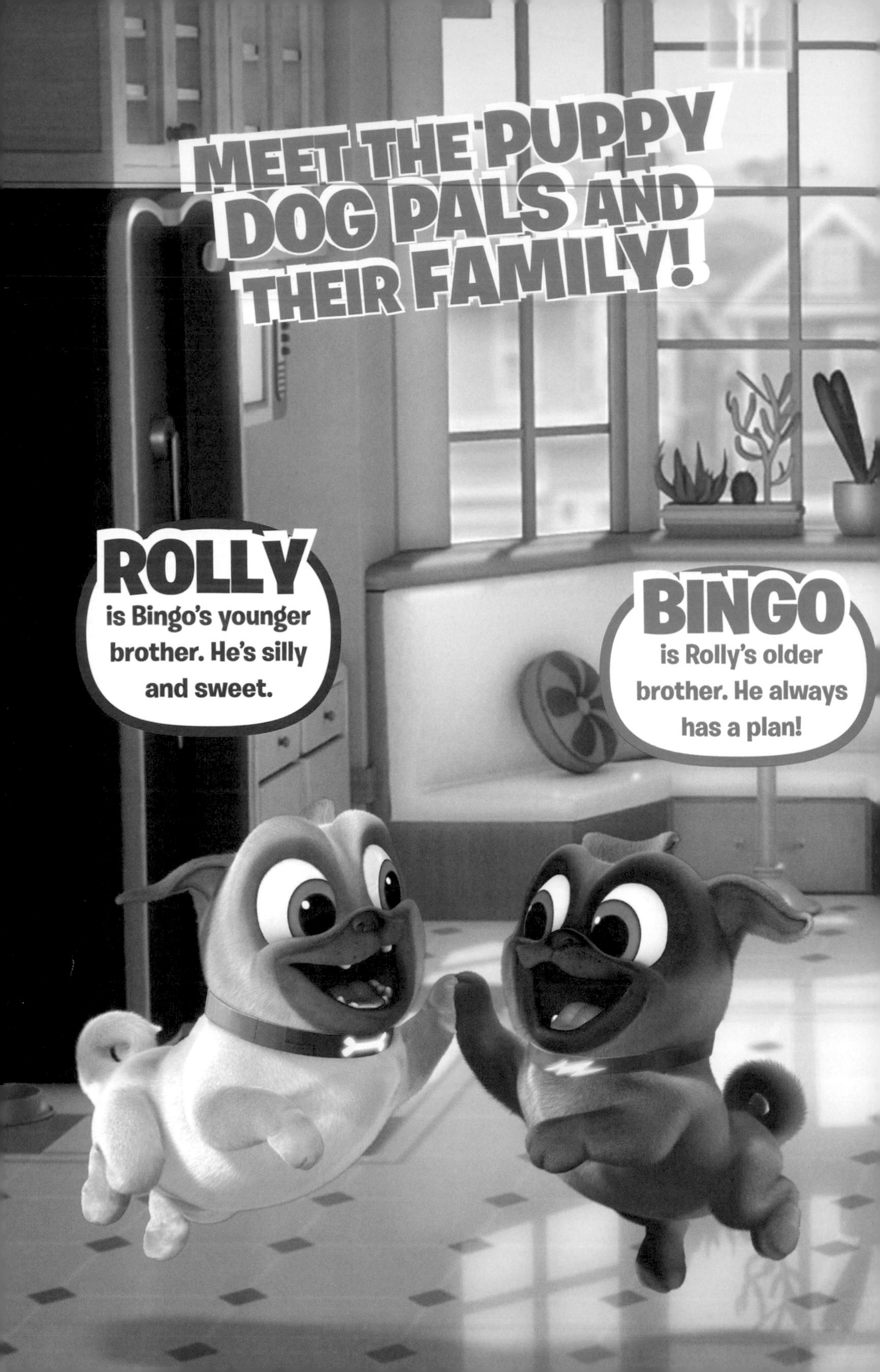

ROLLY

is Bingo's younger brother. He's silly and sweet.

BINGO

is Rolly's older brother. He always has a plan!

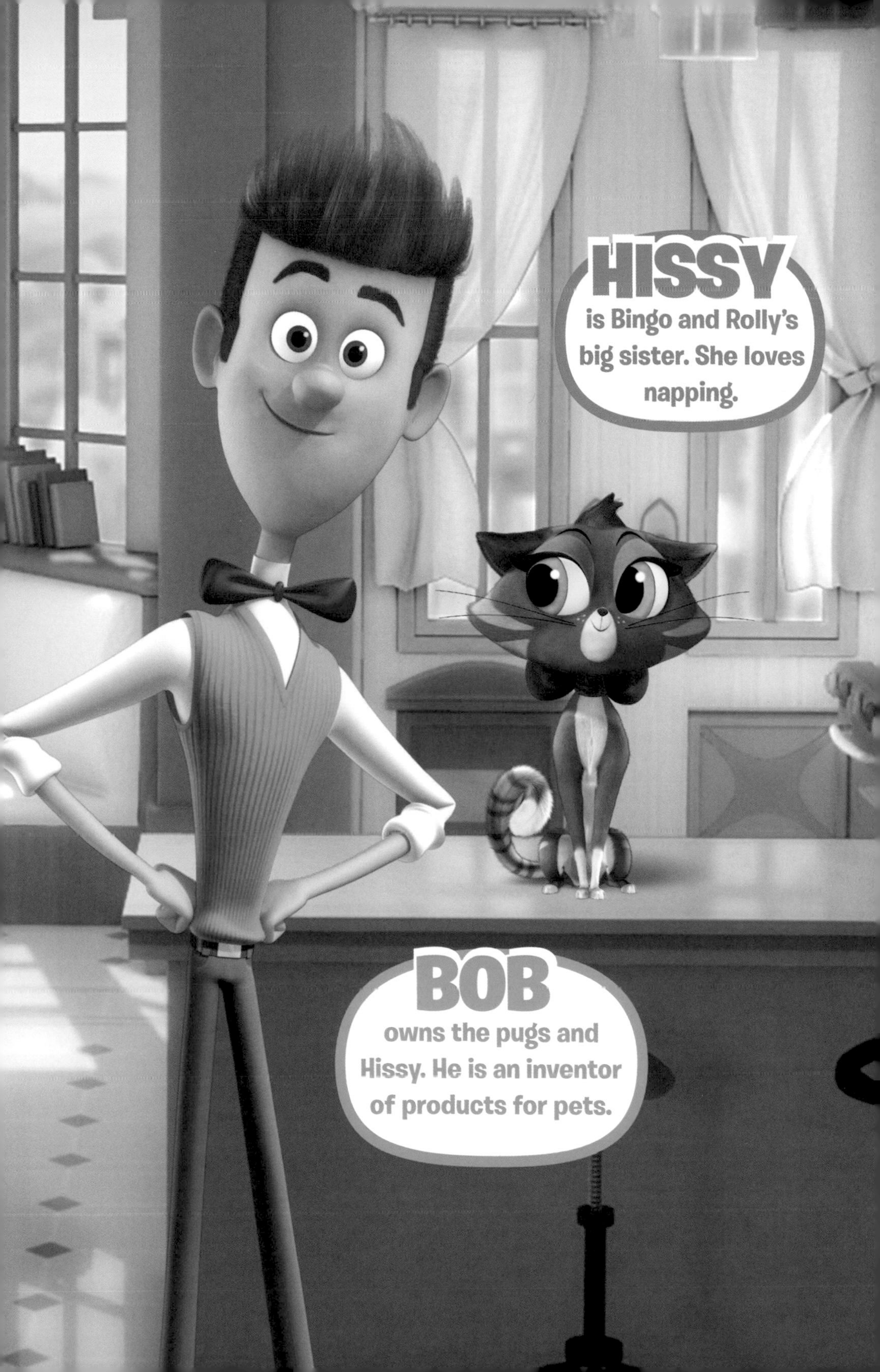
HISSY
is Bingo and Rolly's big sister. She loves napping.
BOB
owns the pugs and Hissy. He is an inventor of products for pets.

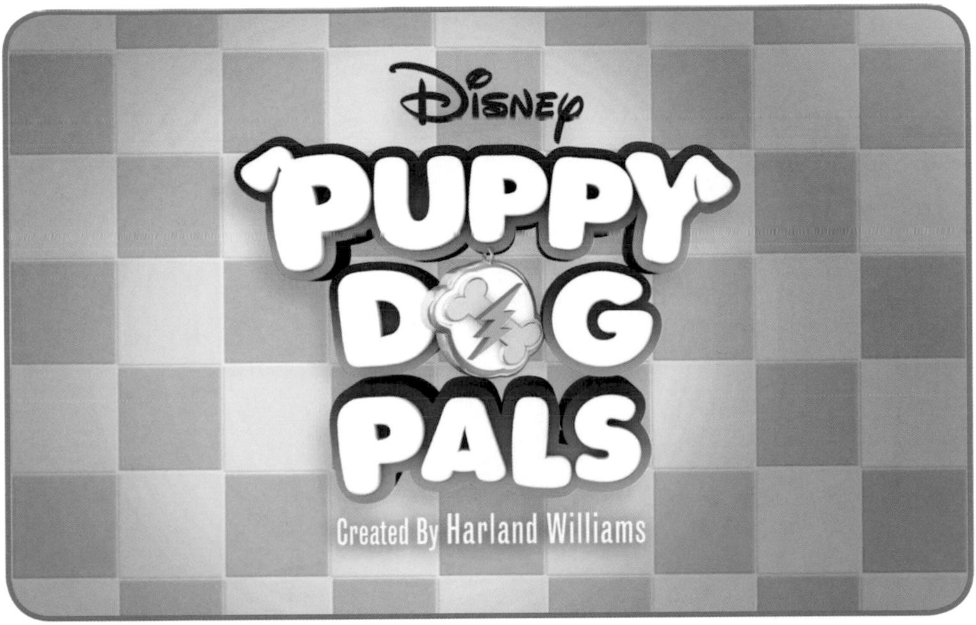
DISNEY
PUPPY DOG PALS
Created By Harland Williams

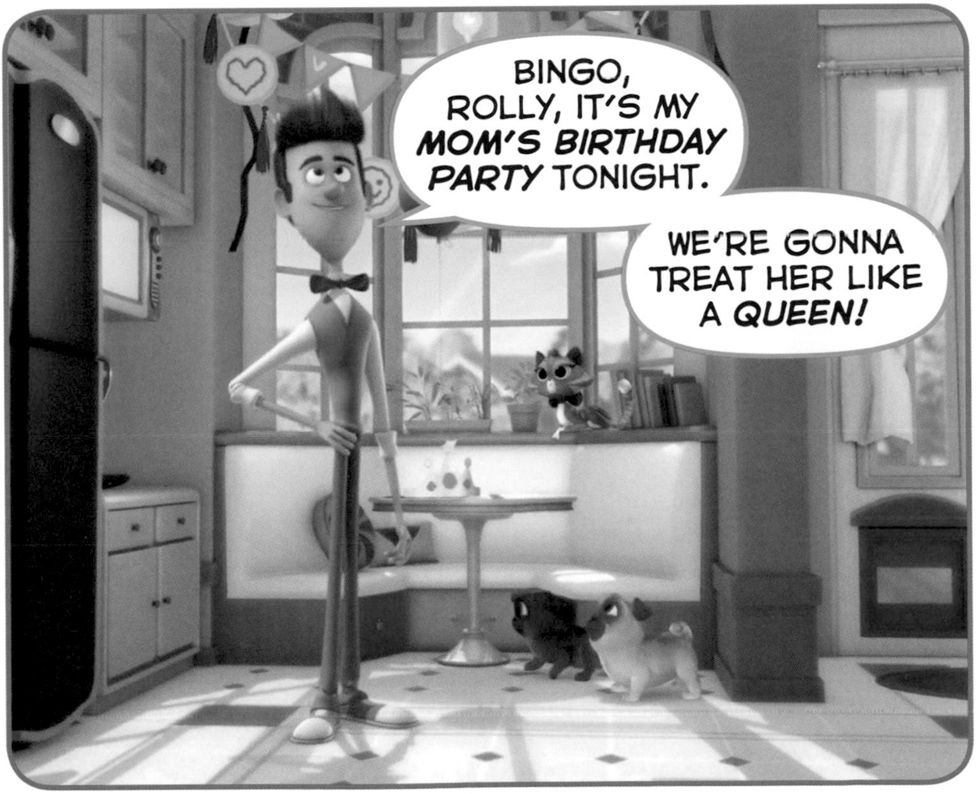
BINGO, ROLLY, IT'S MY *MOM'S BIRTHDAY PARTY* TONIGHT.
WE'RE GONNA TREAT HER LIKE A *QUEEN!*

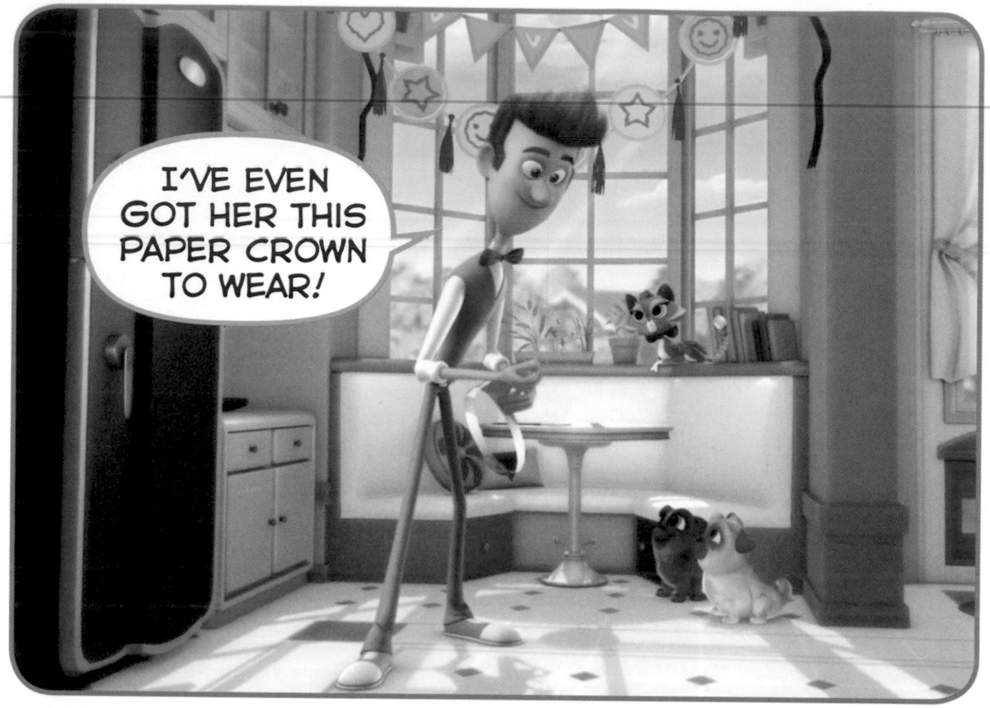
I'VE EVEN GOT HER THIS PAPER CROWN TO WEAR!

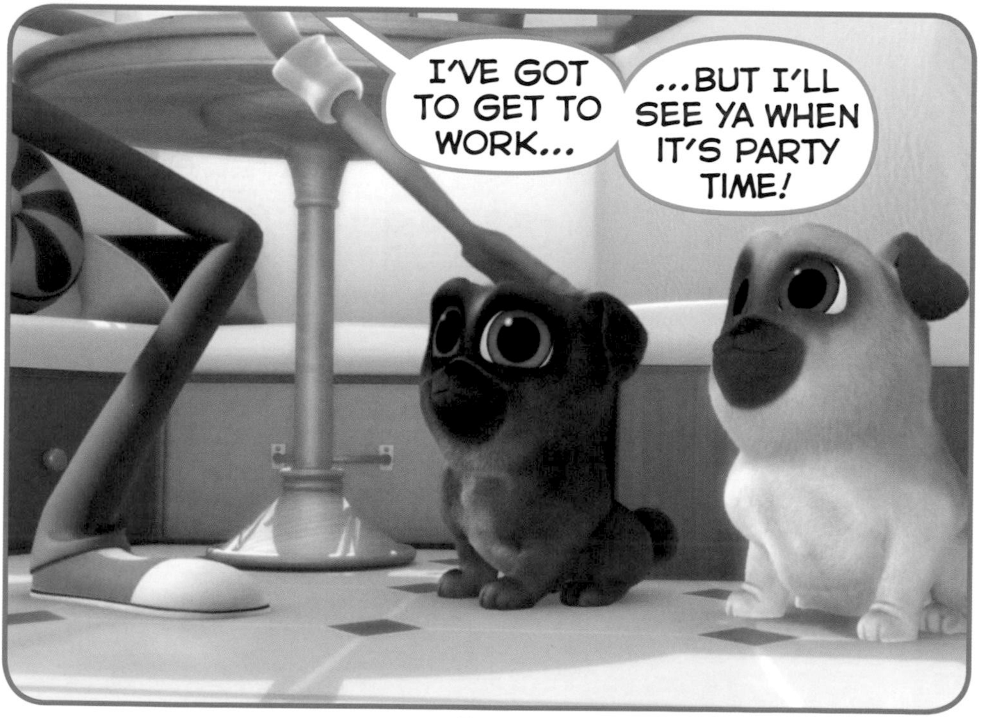
I'VE GOT TO GET TO WORK...
...BUT I'LL SEE YA WHEN IT'S PARTY TIME!

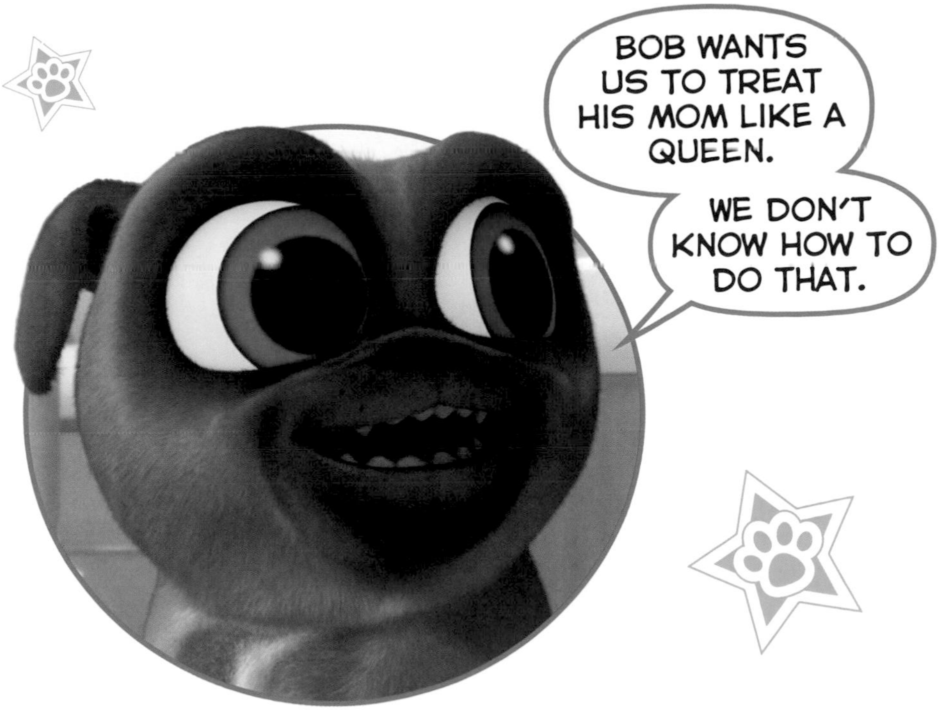
BOB WANTS US TO TREAT HIS MOM LIKE A QUEEN.
WE DON'T KNOW HOW TO DO THAT.

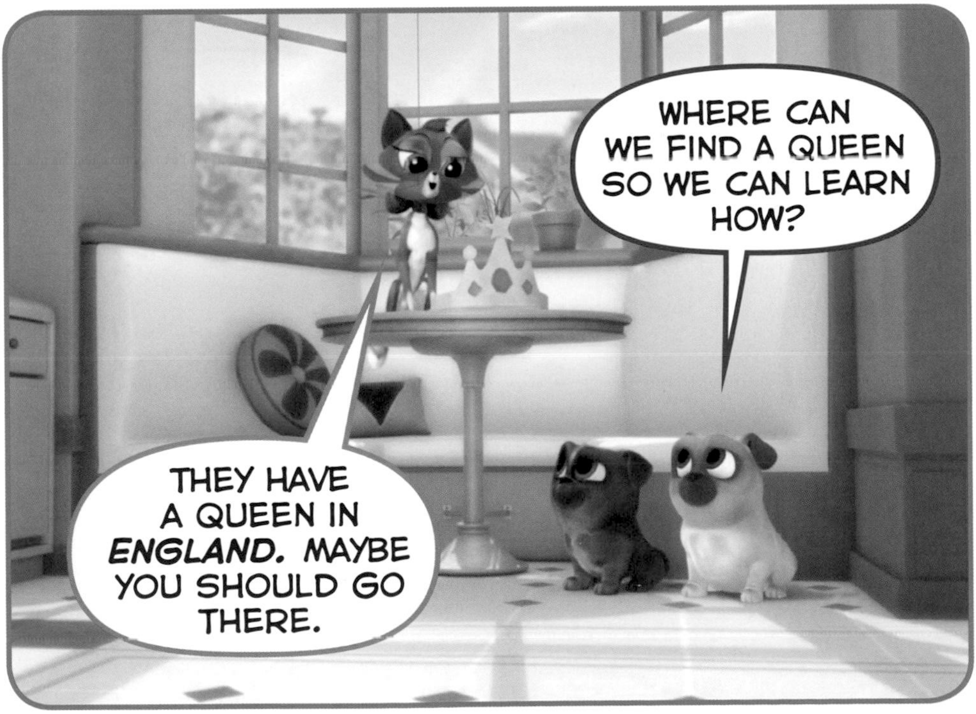
WHERE CAN WE FIND A QUEEN SO WE CAN LEARN HOW?
THEY HAVE A QUEEN IN *ENGLAND.* MAYBE YOU SHOULD GO THERE.

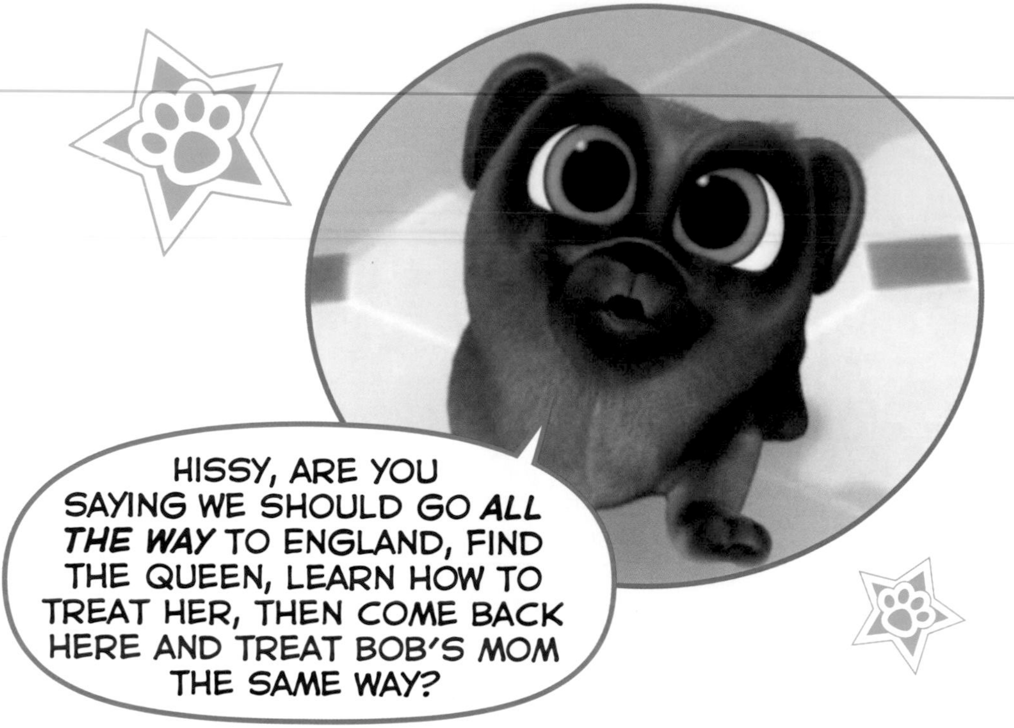
HISSY, ARE YOU SAYING WE SHOULD GO ***ALL THE WAY*** TO ENGLAND, FIND THE QUEEN, LEARN HOW TO TREAT HER, THEN COME BACK HERE AND TREAT BOB'S MOM THE SAME WAY?

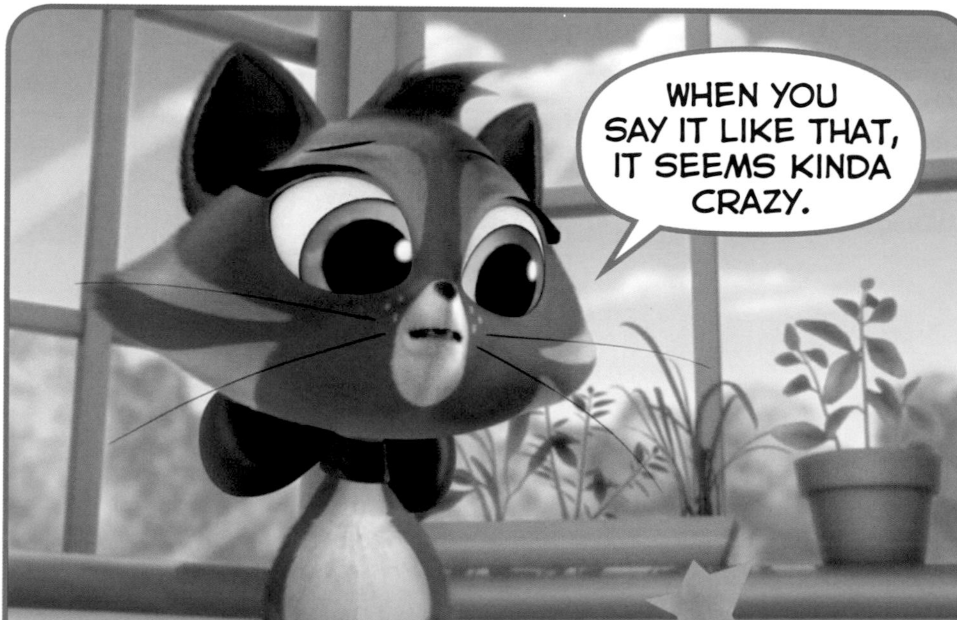
WHEN YOU SAY IT LIKE THAT, IT SEEMS KINDA CRAZY.

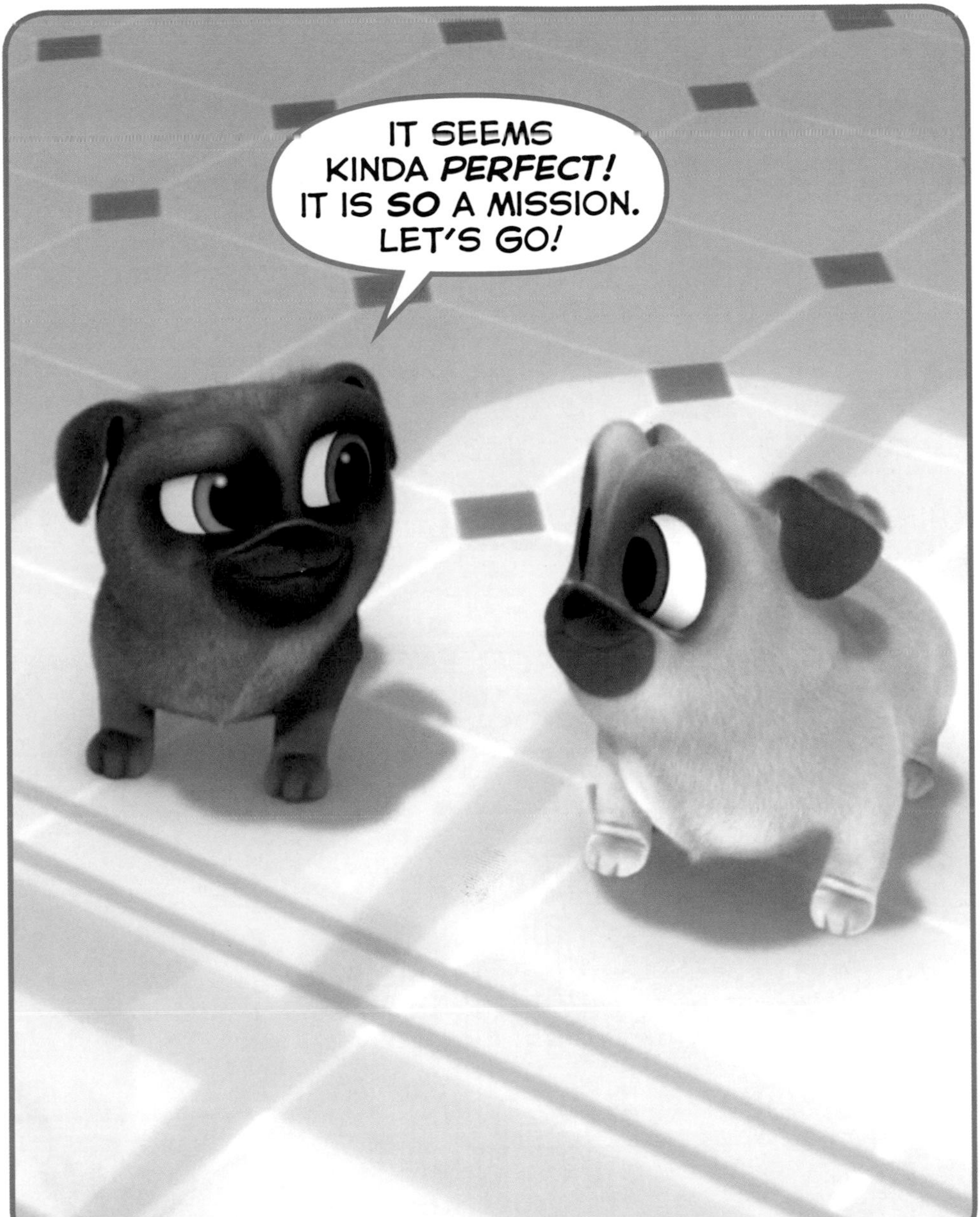
IT SEEMS KINDA *PERFECT!* IT IS **SO** A MISSION. LET'S GO!

BINGO AND ROLLY FLY ACROSS THE OCEAN TO ENGLAND.

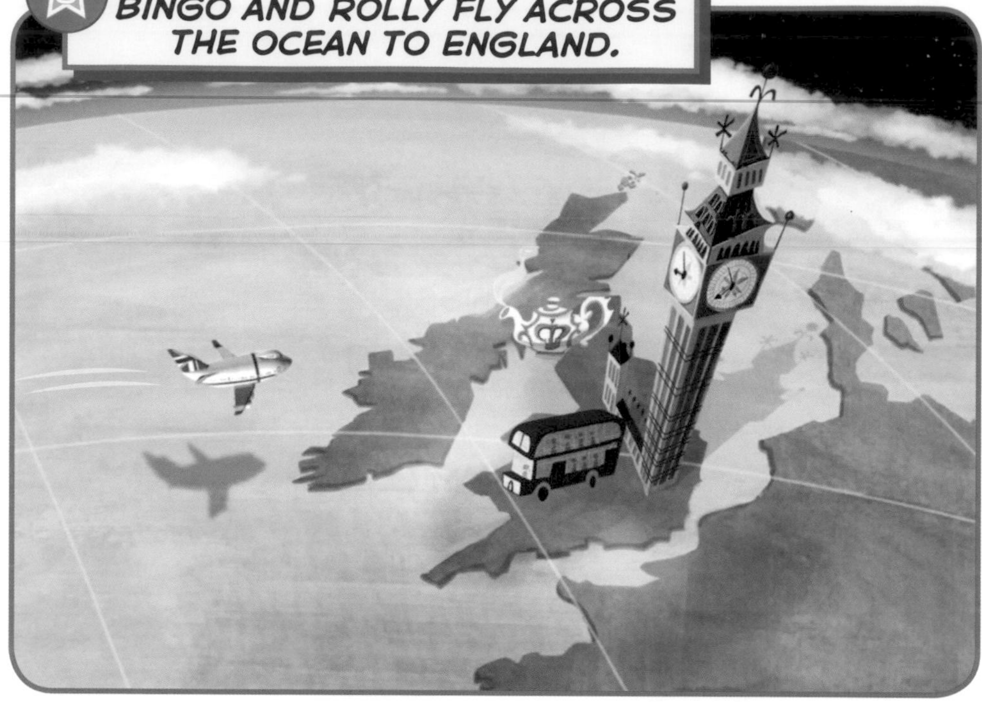

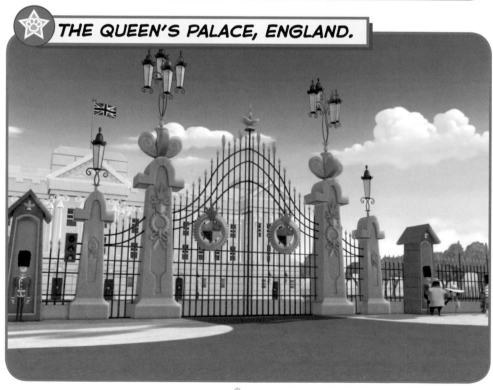

THE QUEEN'S PALACE, ENGLAND.

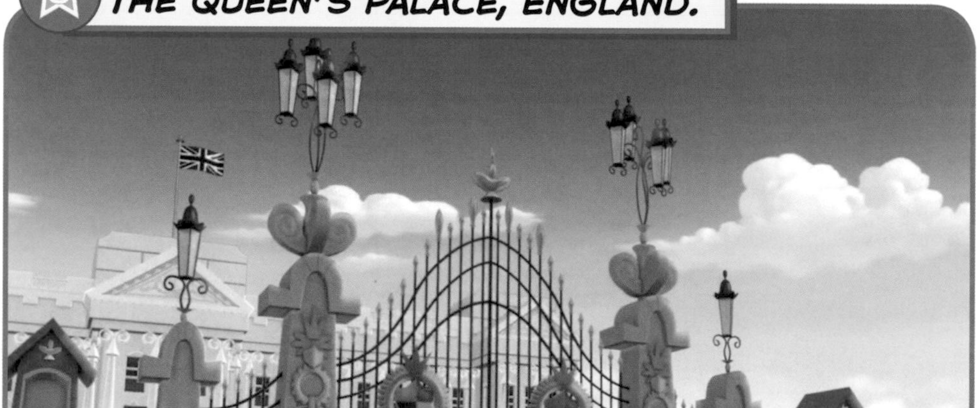

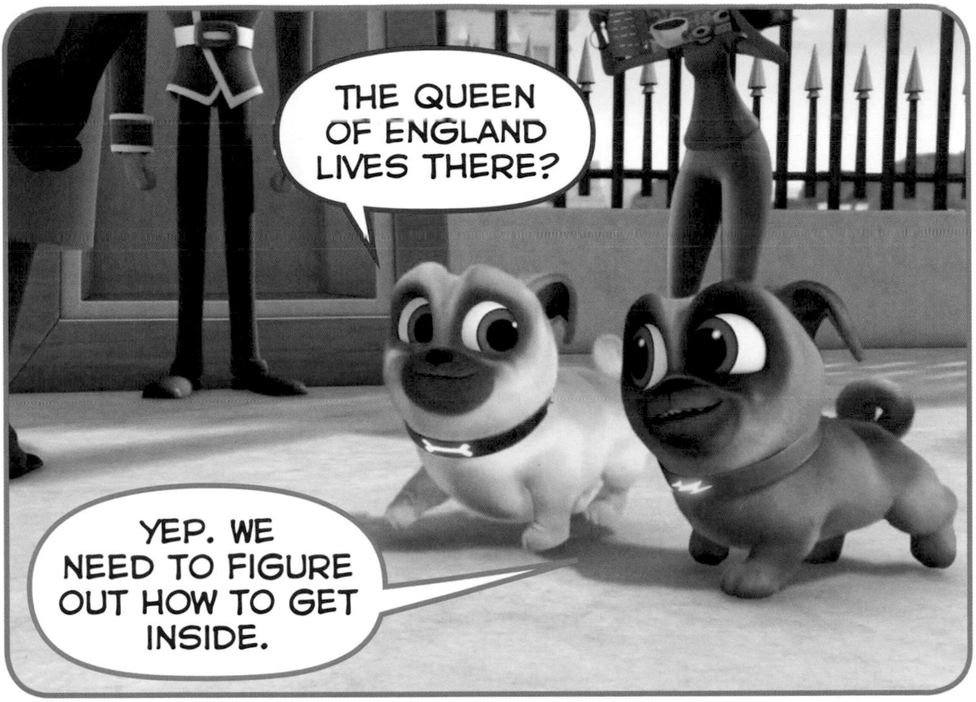
THE QUEEN OF ENGLAND LIVES THERE?
YEP. WE NEED TO FIGURE OUT HOW TO GET INSIDE.

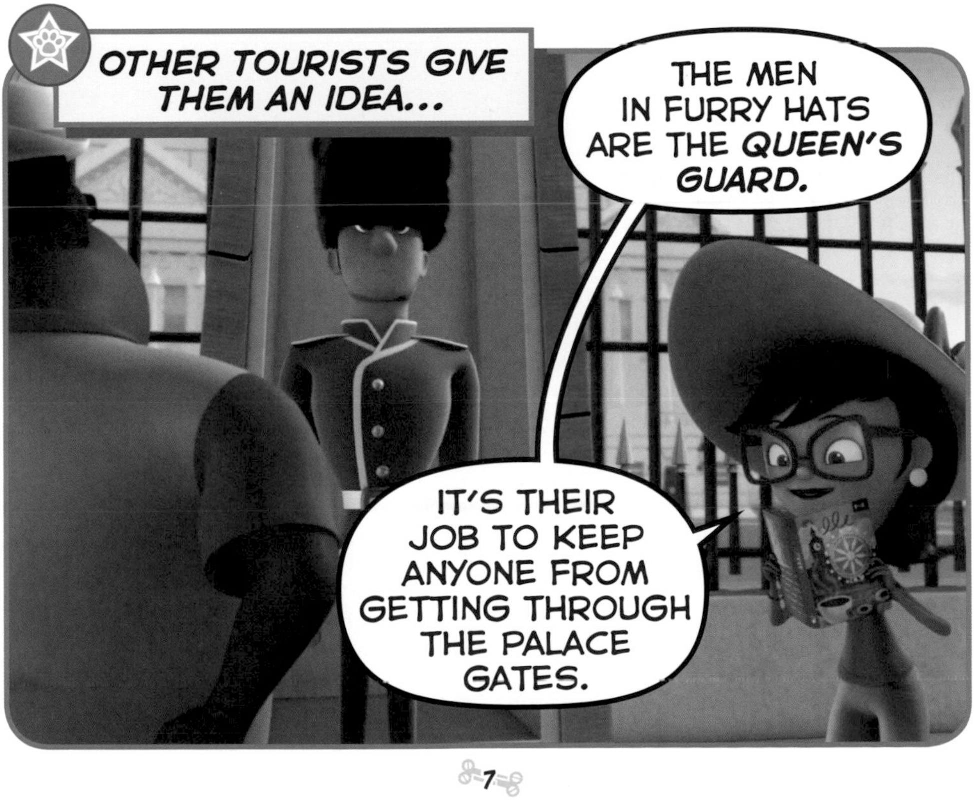
OTHER TOURISTS GIVE THEM AN IDEA...
THE MEN IN FURRY HATS ARE THE QUEEN'S GUARD.
IT'S THEIR JOB TO KEEP ANYONE FROM GETTING THROUGH THE PALACE GATES.

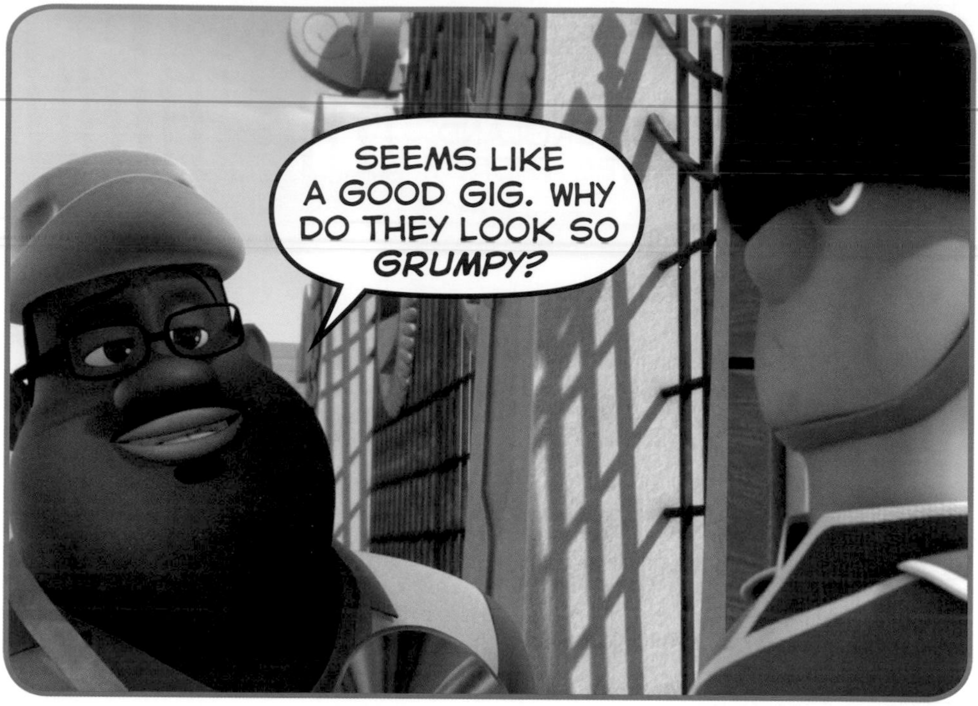
SEEMS LIKE A GOOD GIG. WHY DO THEY LOOK SO *GRUMPY?*

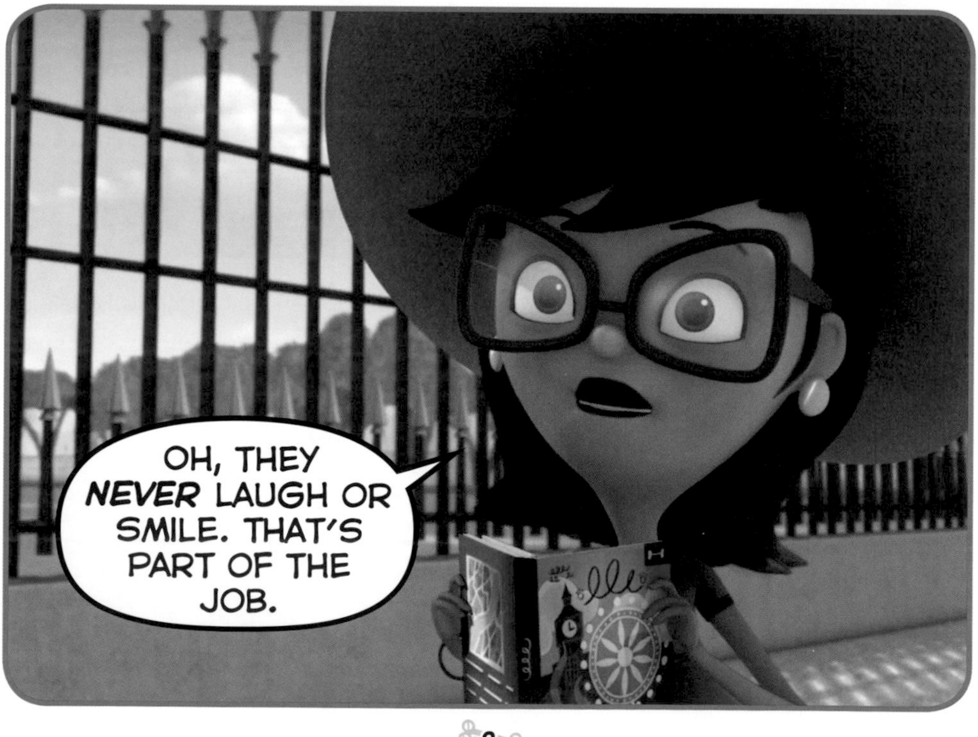
OH, THEY ***NEVER*** LAUGH OR SMILE. THAT'S PART OF THE JOB.

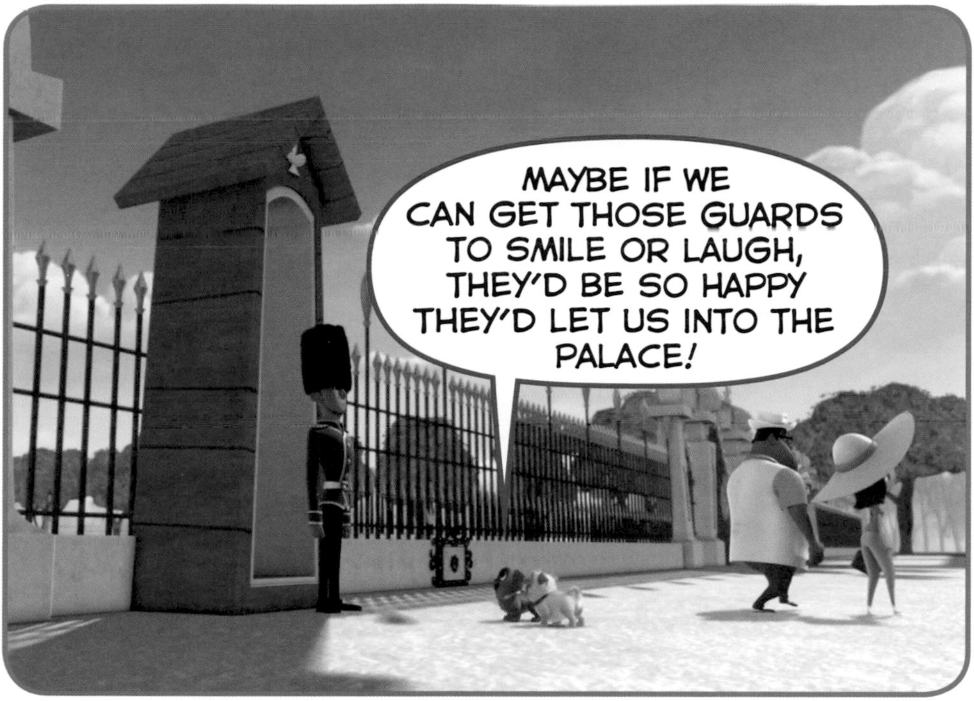
MAYBE IF WE CAN GET THOSE GUARDS TO SMILE OR LAUGH, THEY'D BE SO HAPPY THEY'D LET US INTO THE PALACE!

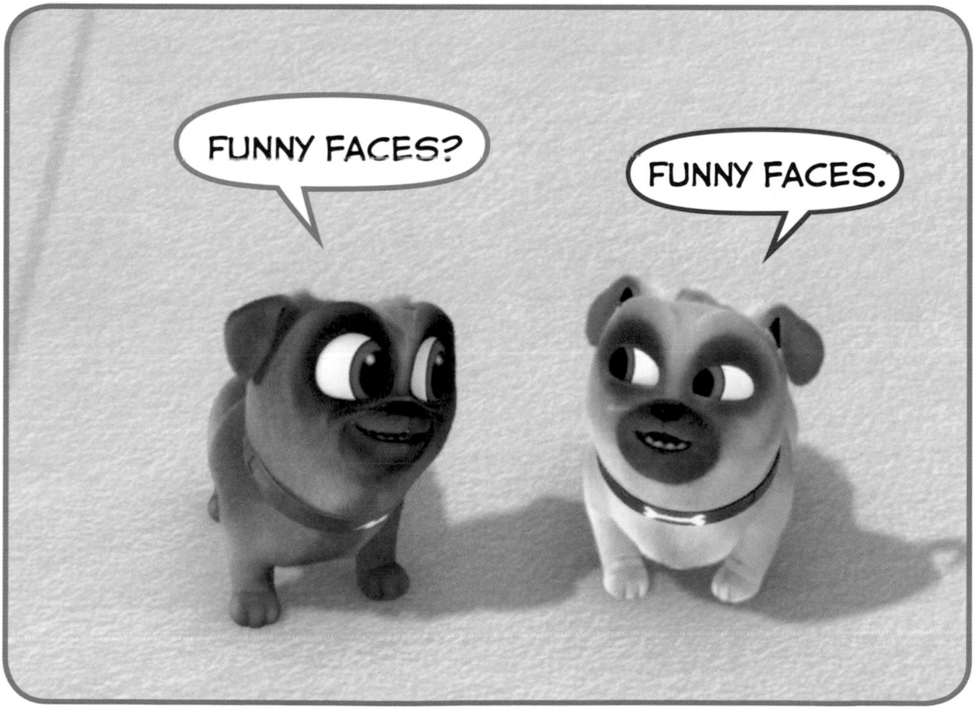
FUNNY FACES?
FUNNY FACES.

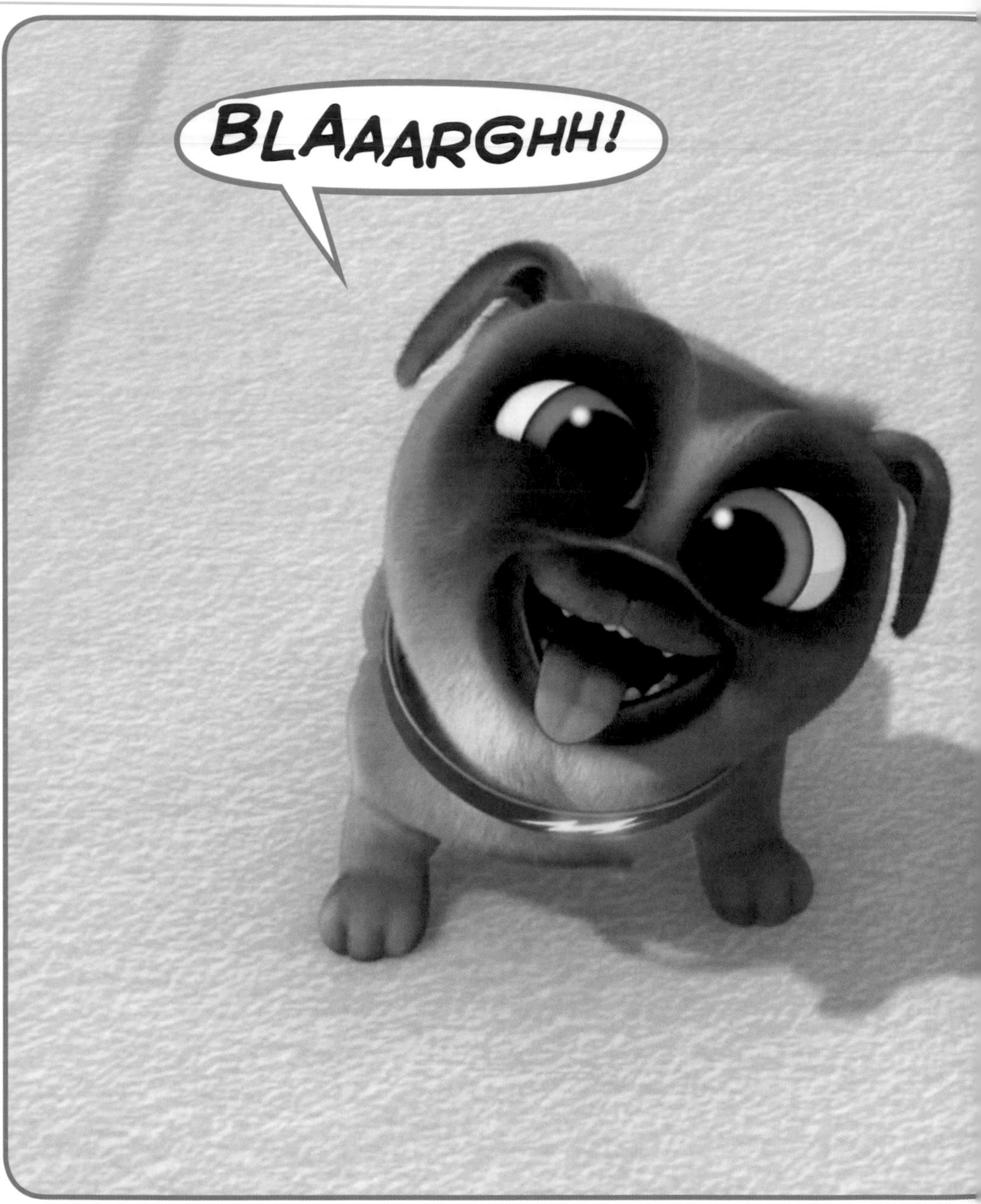
BLAAARGHH!

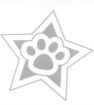

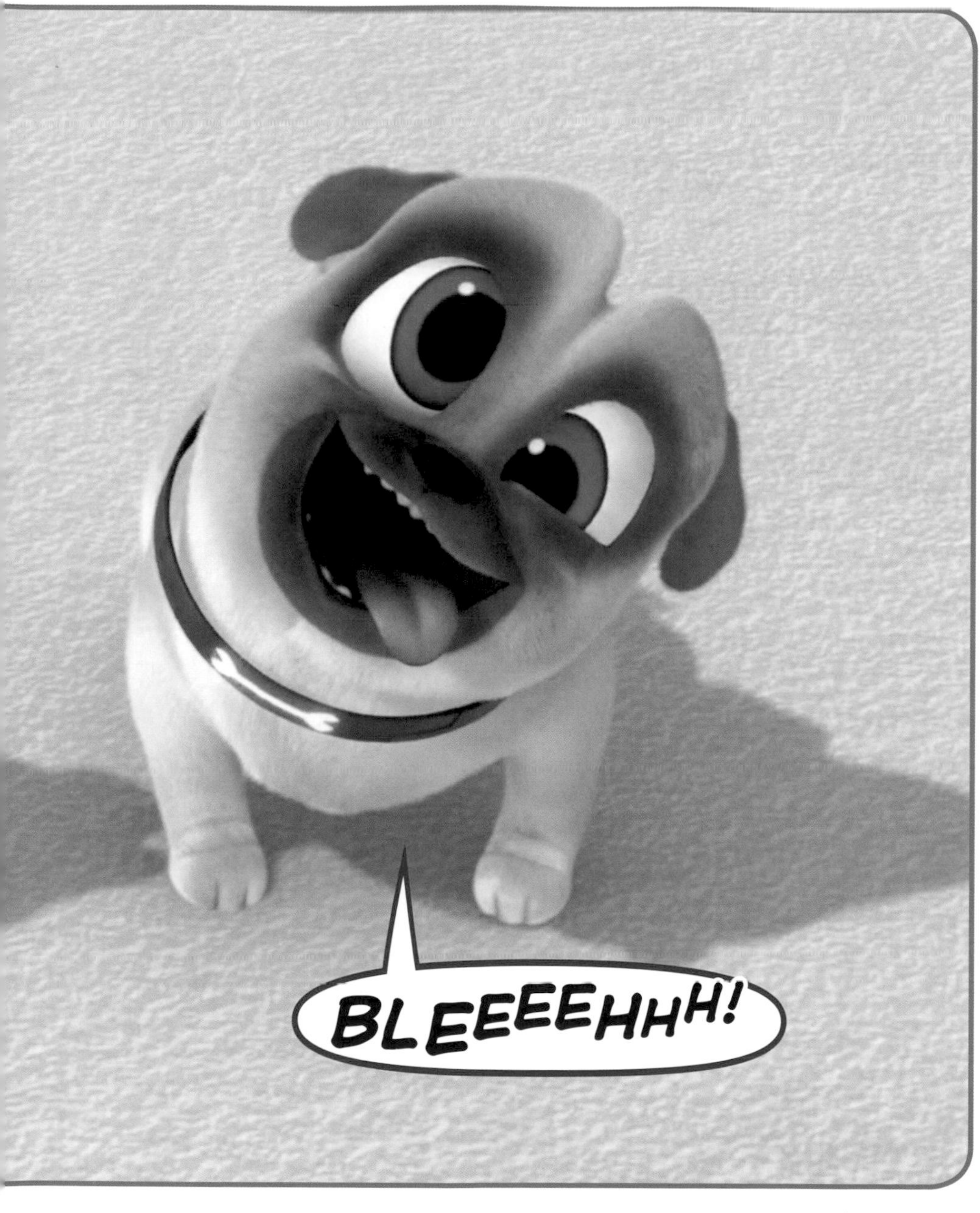
BLEEEEEHHH!

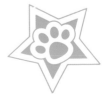

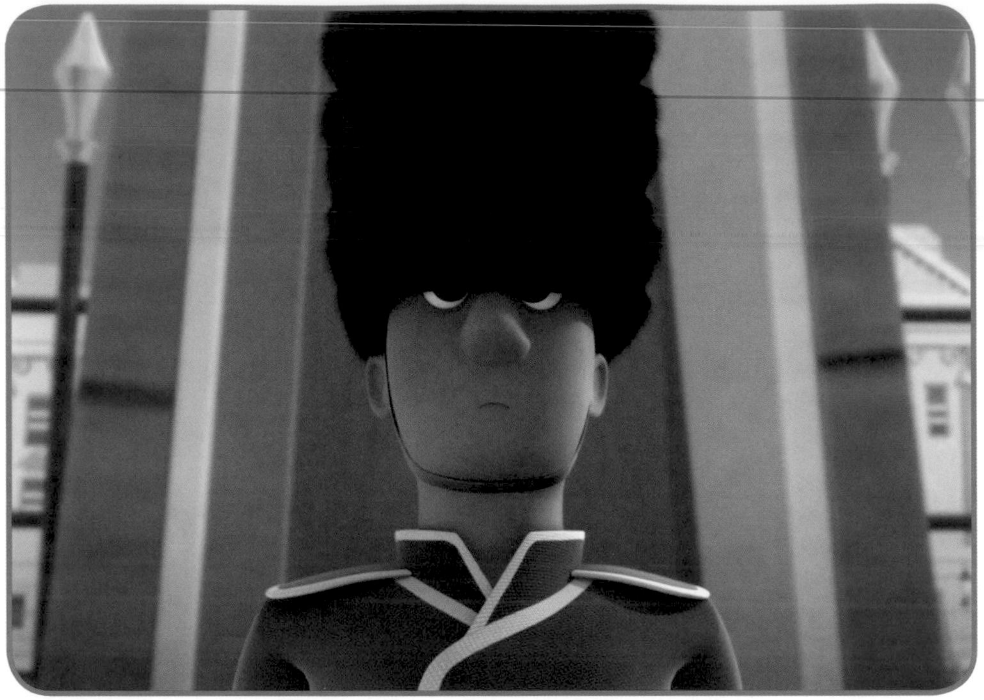

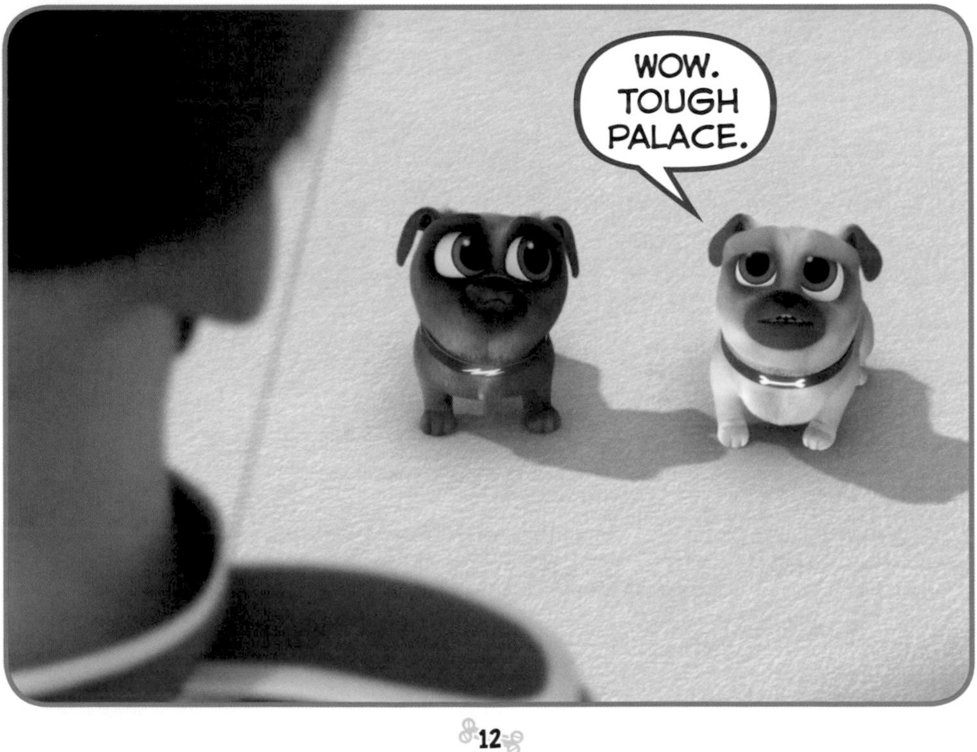
WOW. TOUGH PALACE.

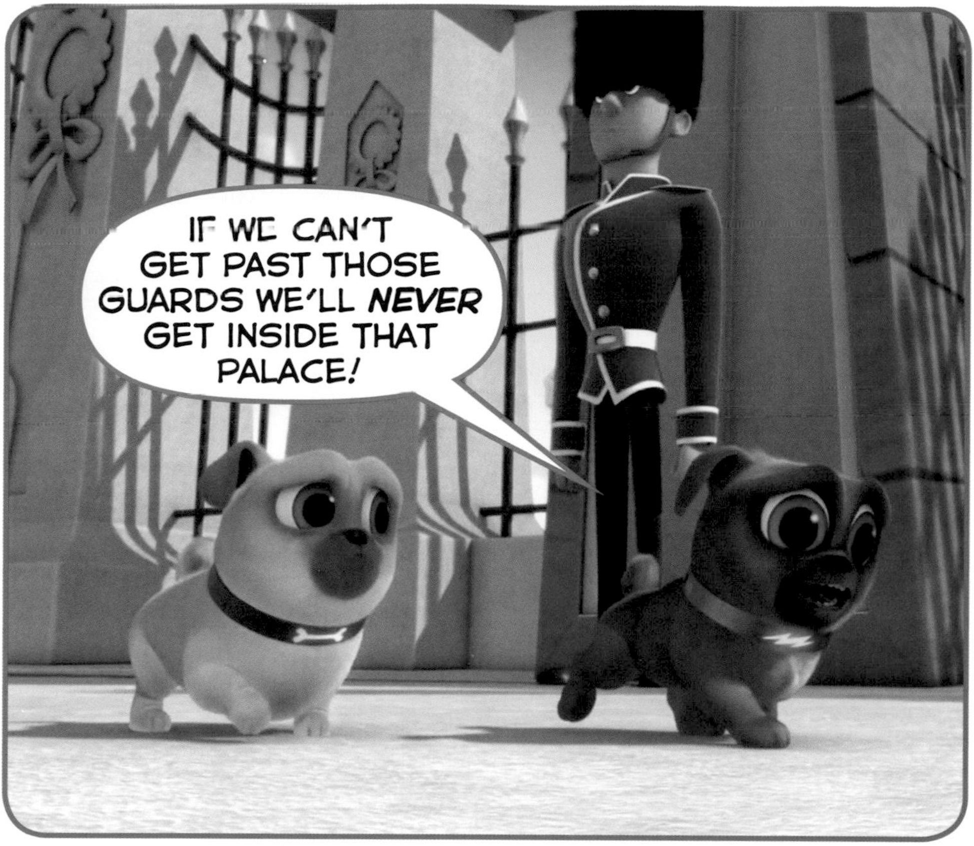
IF WE CAN'T GET PAST THOSE GUARDS WE'LL NEVER GET INSIDE THAT PALACE!

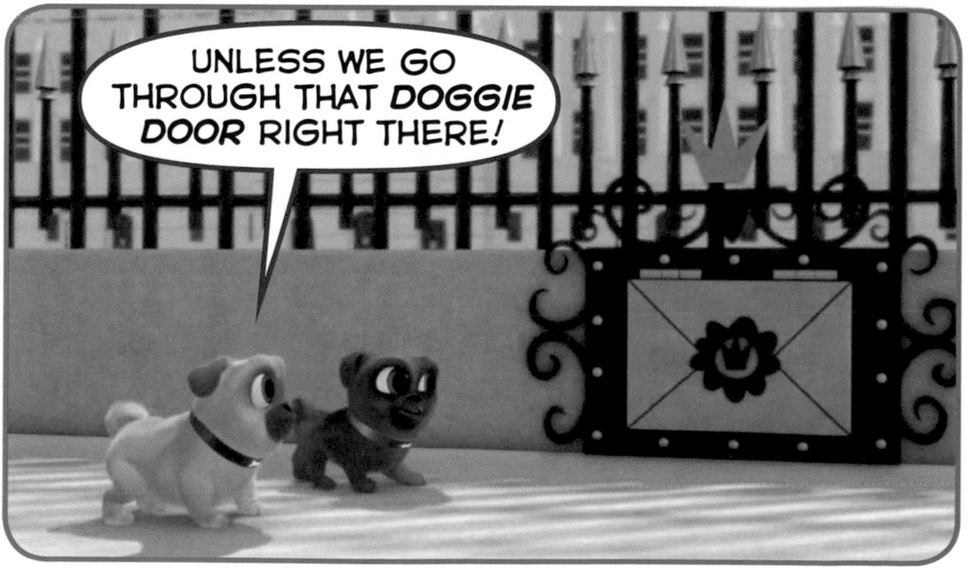
UNLESS WE GO THROUGH THAT DOGGIE DOOR RIGHT THERE!

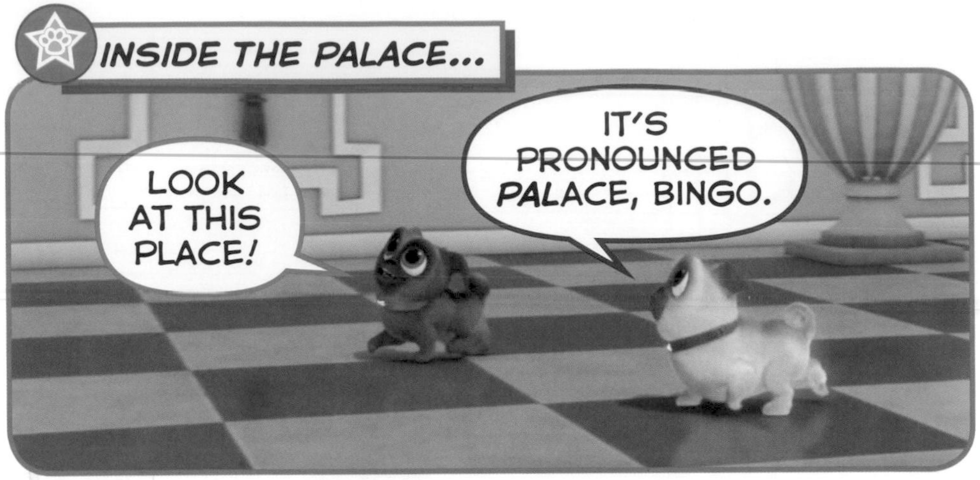
INSIDE THE PALACE...
LOOK AT THIS PLACE!
IT'S PRONOUNCED PALACE, BINGO.

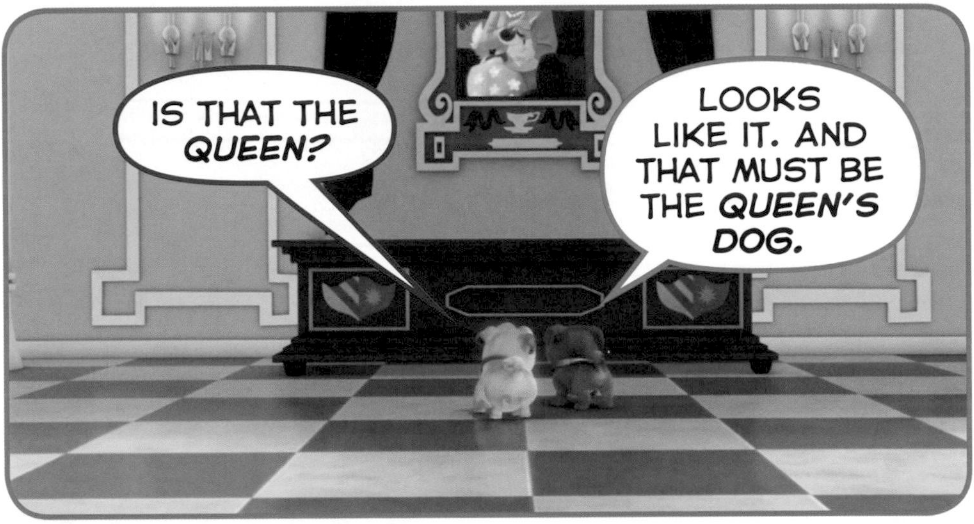
IS THAT THE QUEEN?
LOOKS LIKE IT. AND THAT MUST BE THE QUEEN'S DOG.

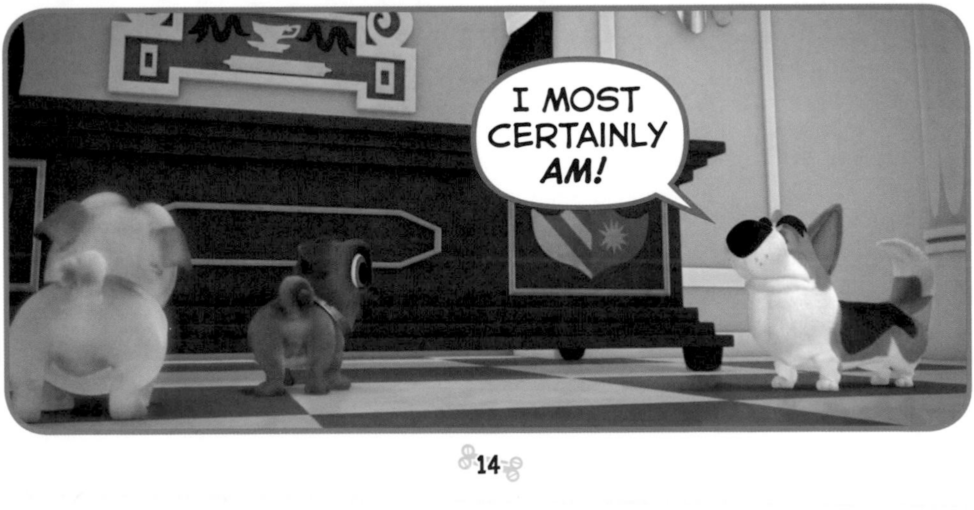
I MOST CERTAINLY AM!

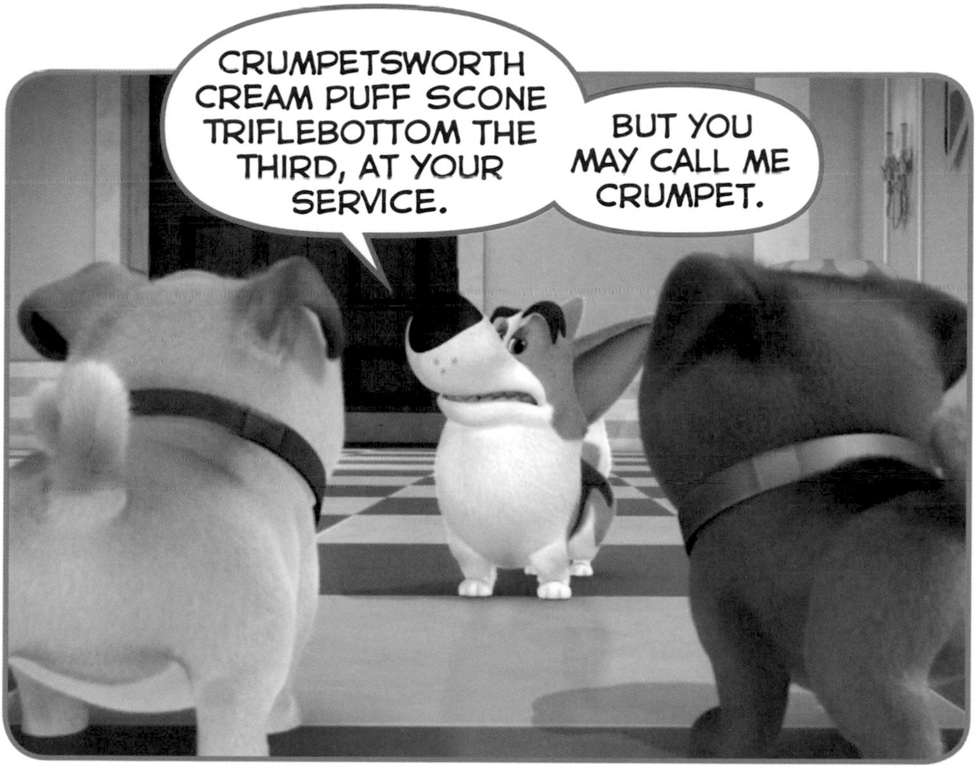
CRUMPETSWORTH CREAM PUFF SCONE TRIFLEBOTTOM THE THIRD, AT YOUR SERVICE.
BUT YOU MAY CALL ME CRUMPET.

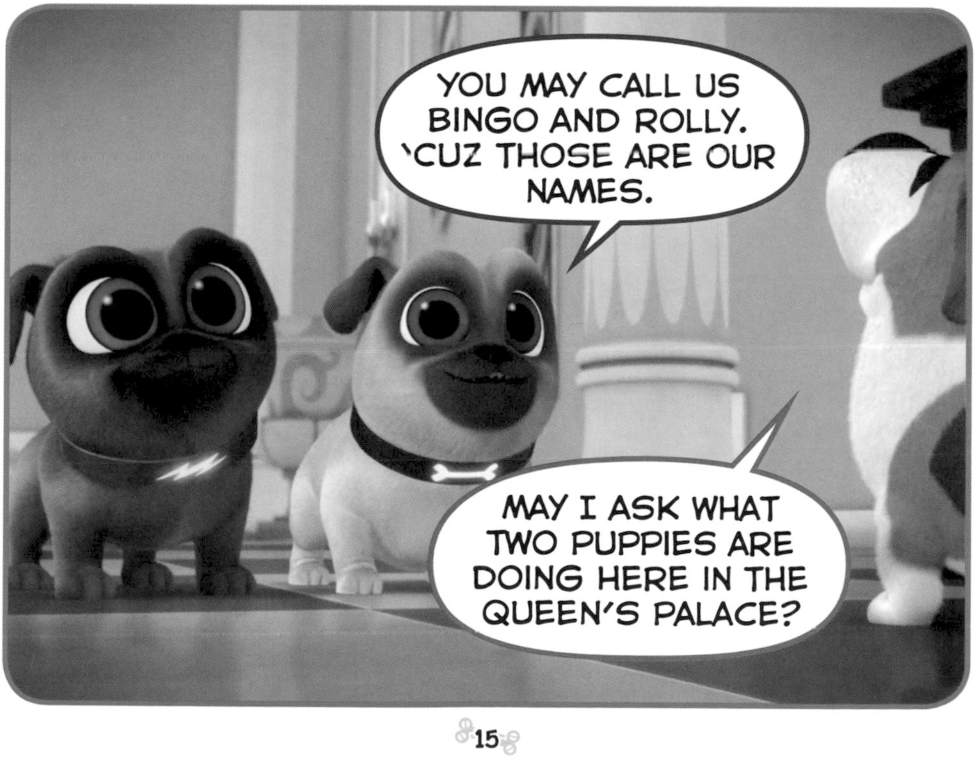
YOU MAY CALL US BINGO AND ROLLY. 'CUZ THOSE ARE OUR NAMES.
MAY I ASK WHAT TWO PUPPIES ARE DOING HERE IN THE QUEEN'S PALACE?

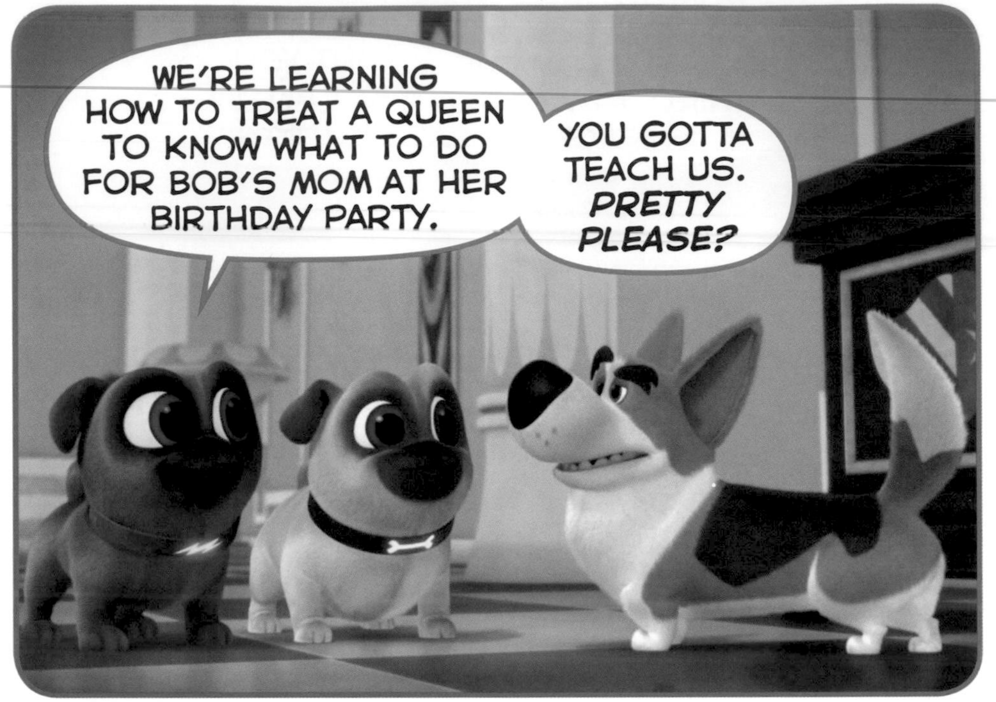
WE'RE LEARNING HOW TO TREAT A QUEEN TO KNOW WHAT TO DO FOR BOB'S MOM AT HER BIRTHDAY PARTY.
YOU GOTTA TEACH US. *PRETTY PLEASE?*

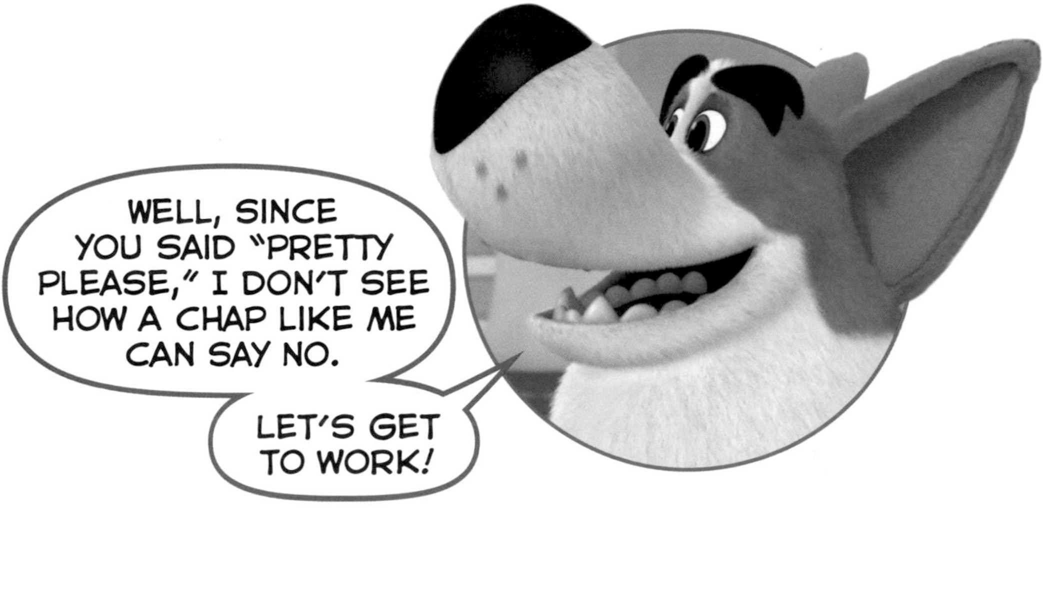
WELL, SINCE YOU SAID "PRETTY PLEASE," I DON'T SEE HOW A CHAP LIKE ME CAN SAY NO.
LET'S GET TO WORK!

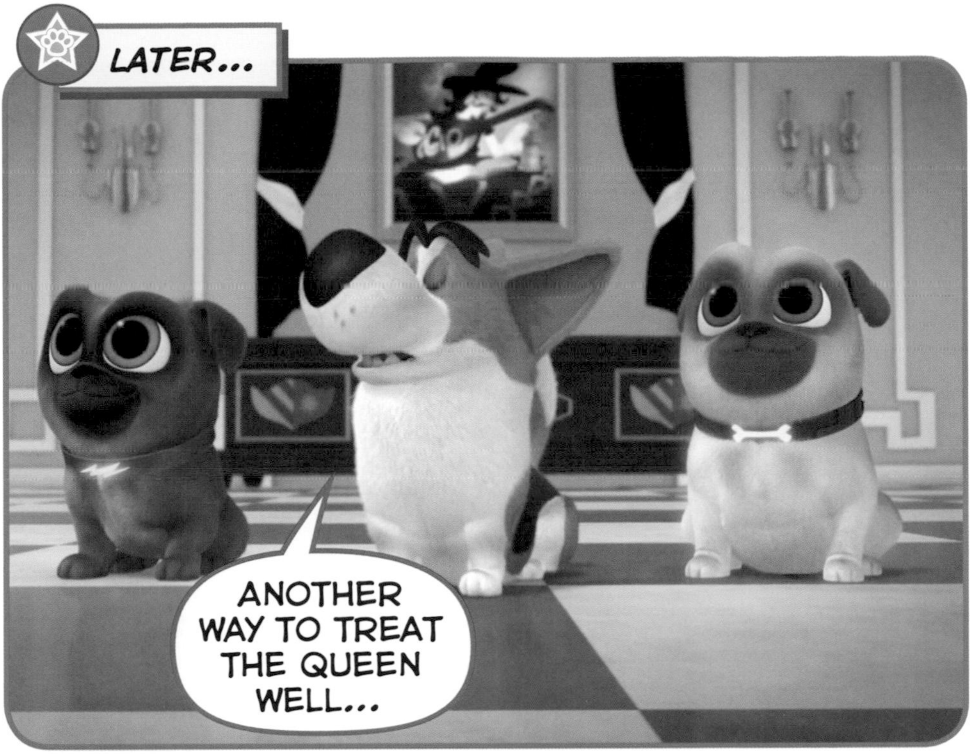
LATER...
ANOTHER WAY TO TREAT THE QUEEN WELL...

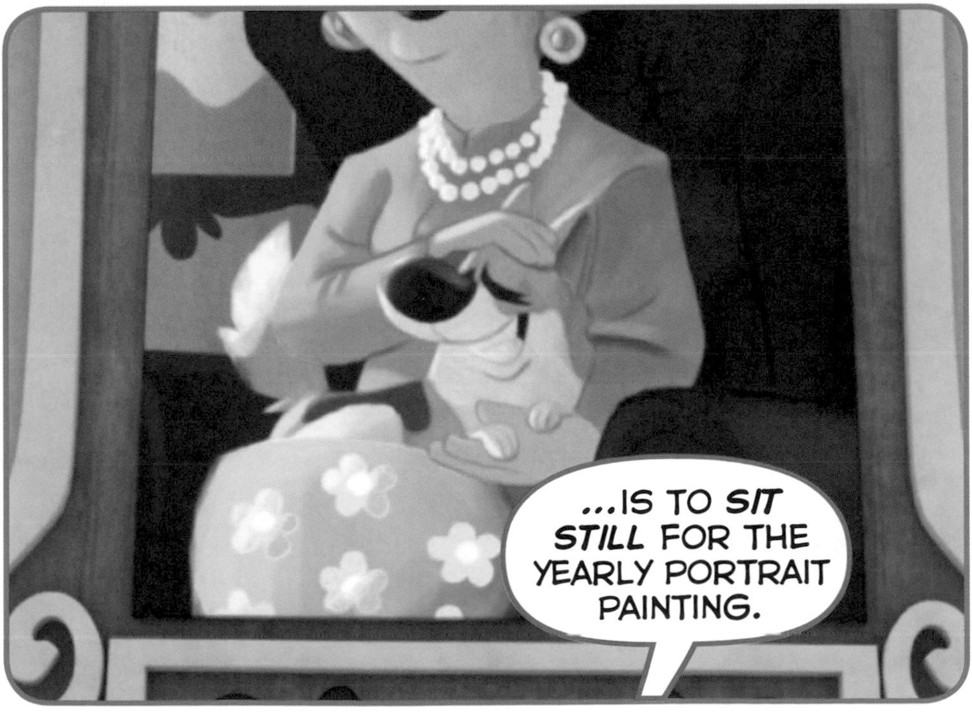
...IS TO *SIT STILL* FOR THE YEARLY PORTRAIT PAINTING.

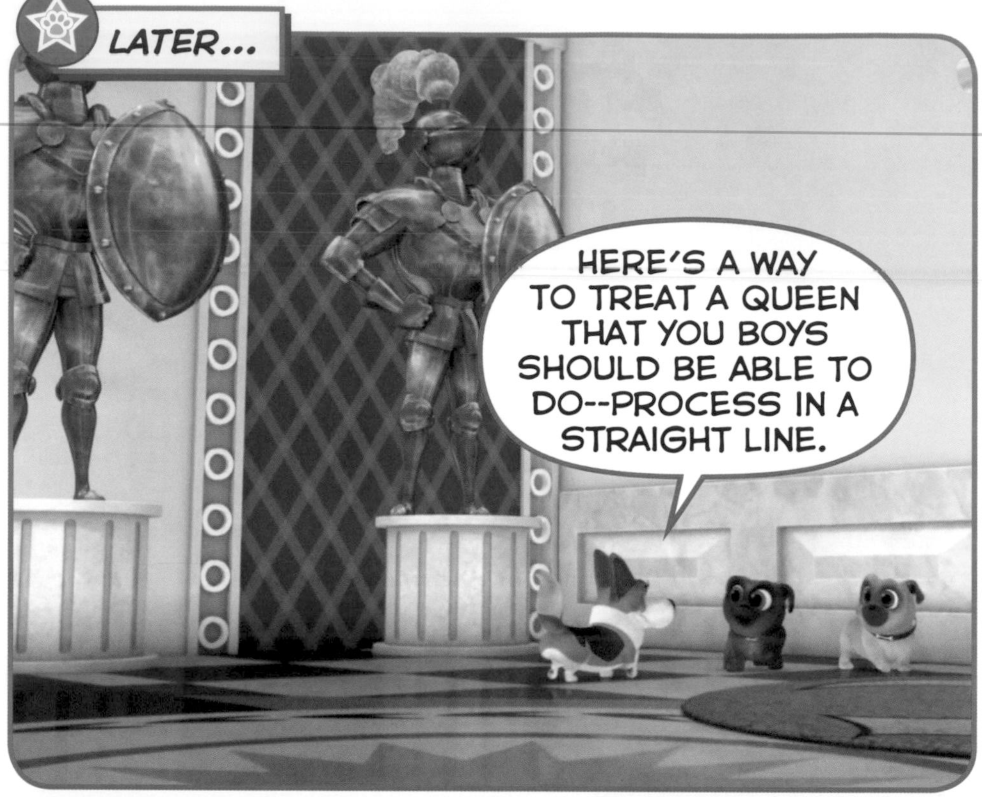
LATER...
HERE'S A WAY TO TREAT A QUEEN THAT YOU BOYS SHOULD BE ABLE TO DO--PROCESS IN A STRAIGHT LINE.

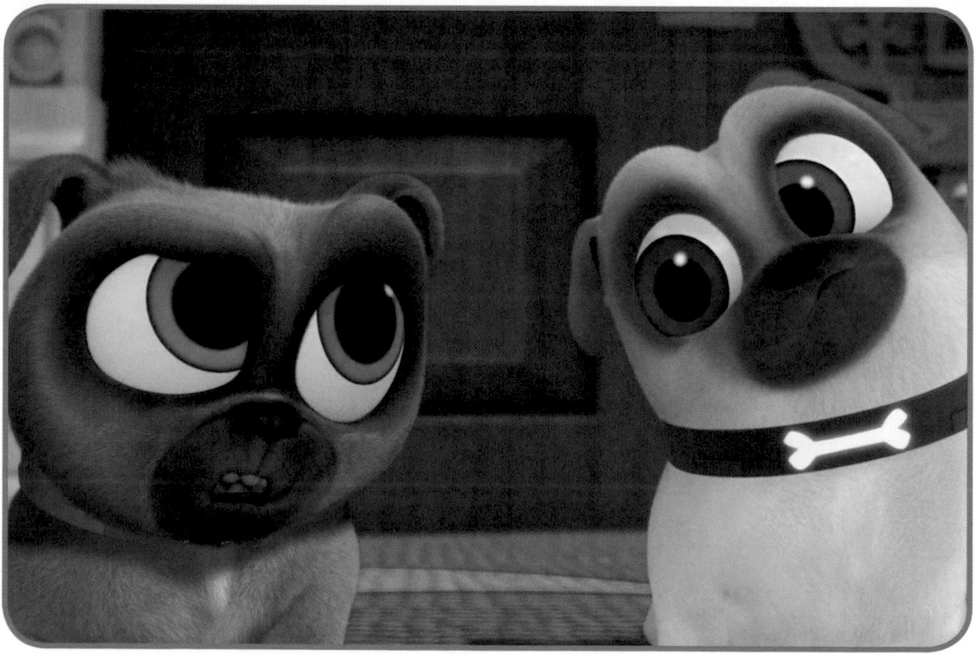

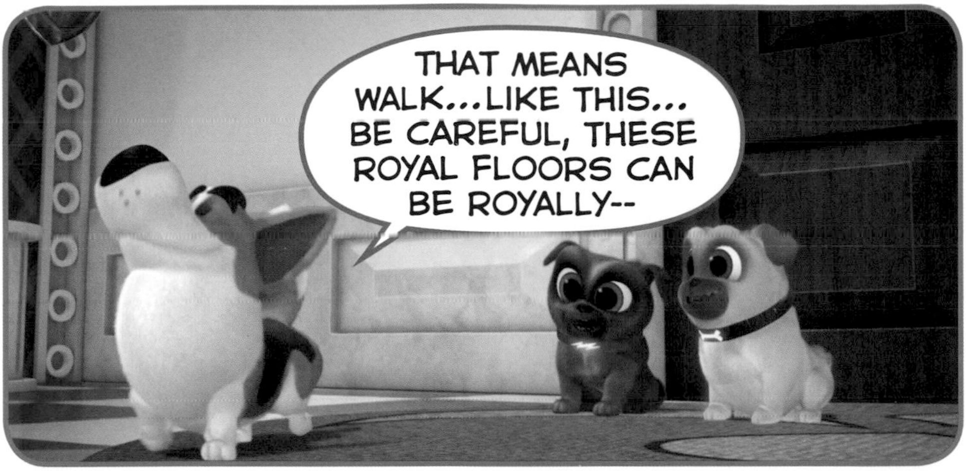
THAT MEANS WALK...LIKE THIS... BE CAREFUL, THESE ROYAL FLOORS CAN BE ROYALLY--

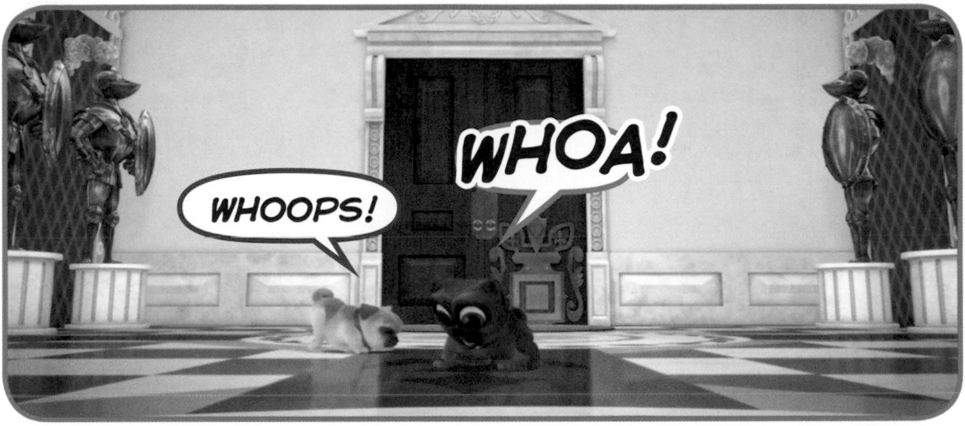
WHOOPS!
WHOA!

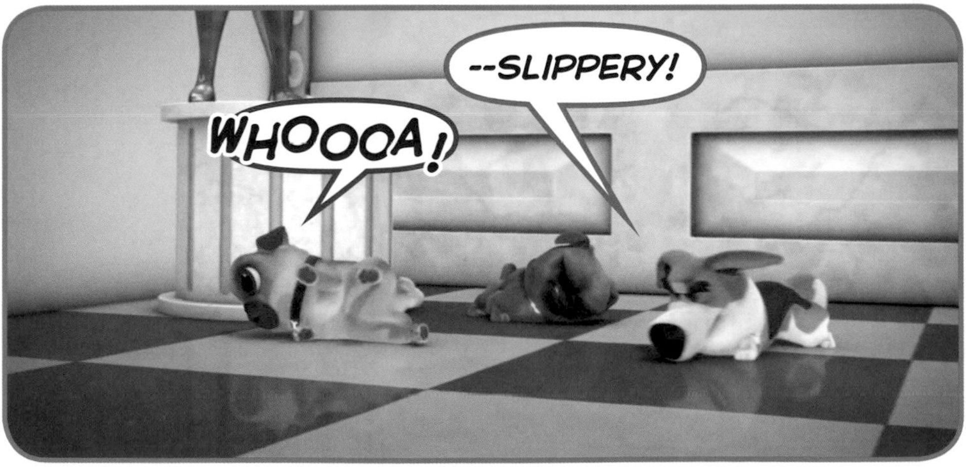
WHOOOA!
--SLIPPERY!

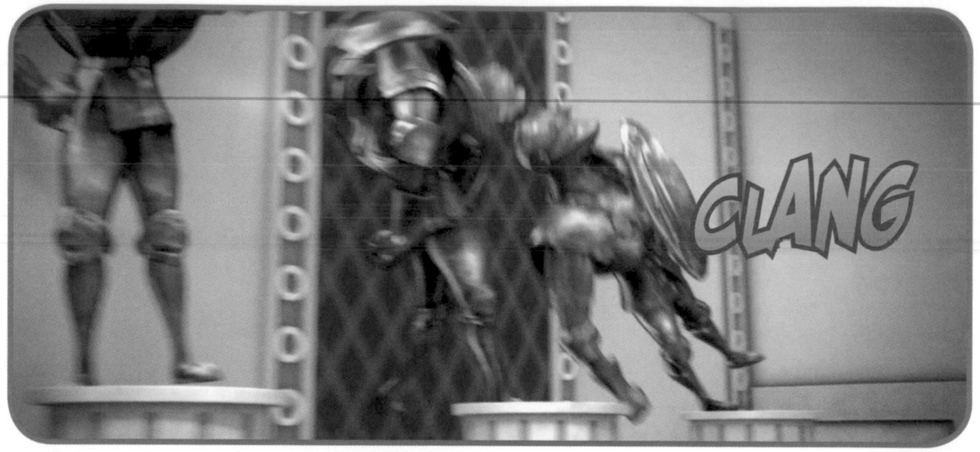
CLANG

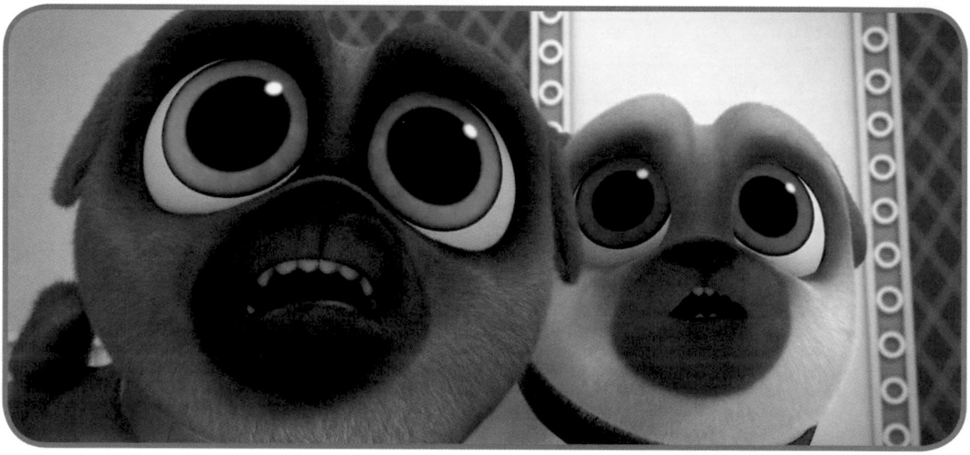

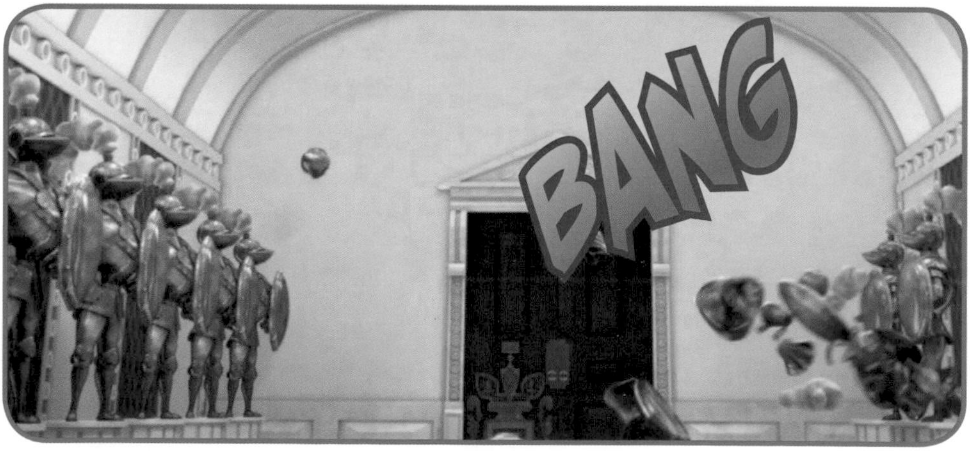
BANG

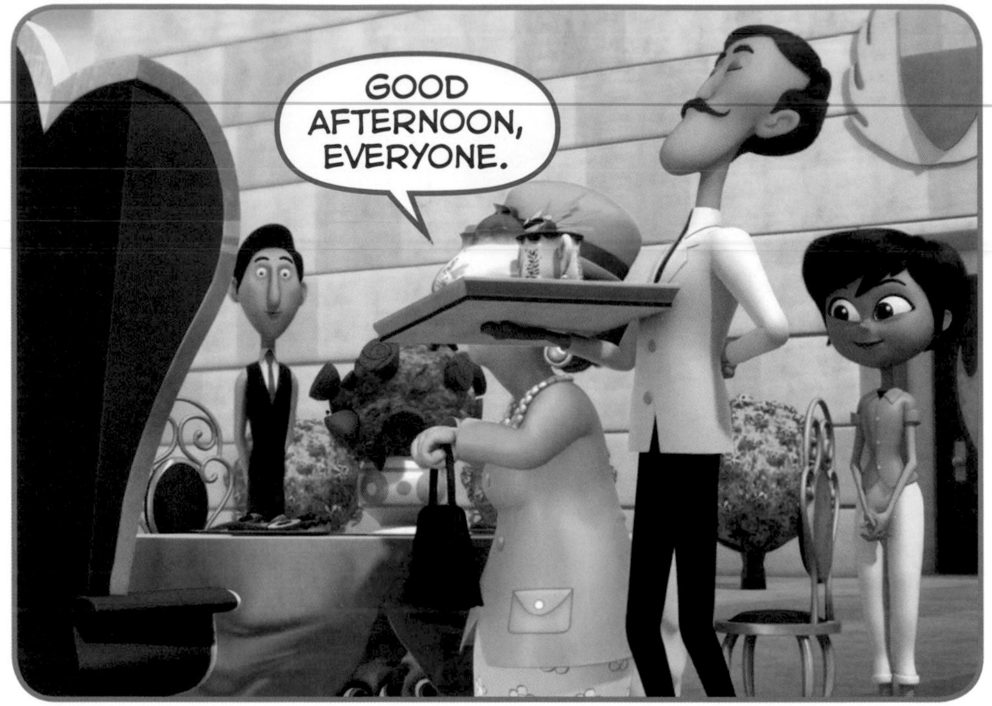
GOOD AFTERNOON, EVERYONE.

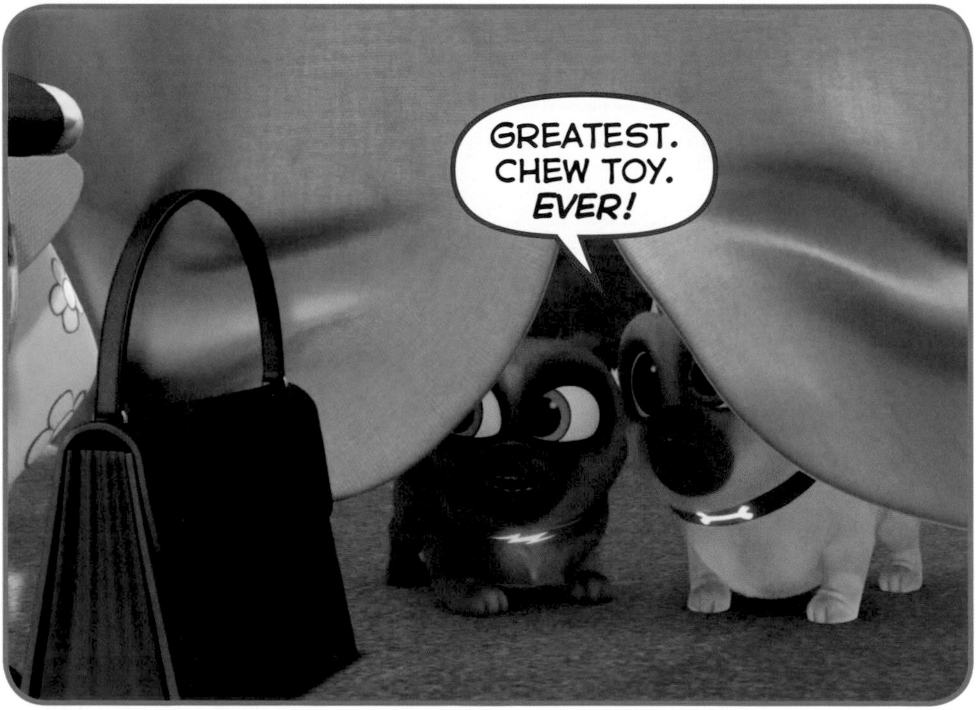
GREATEST. CHEW TOY. *EVER!*

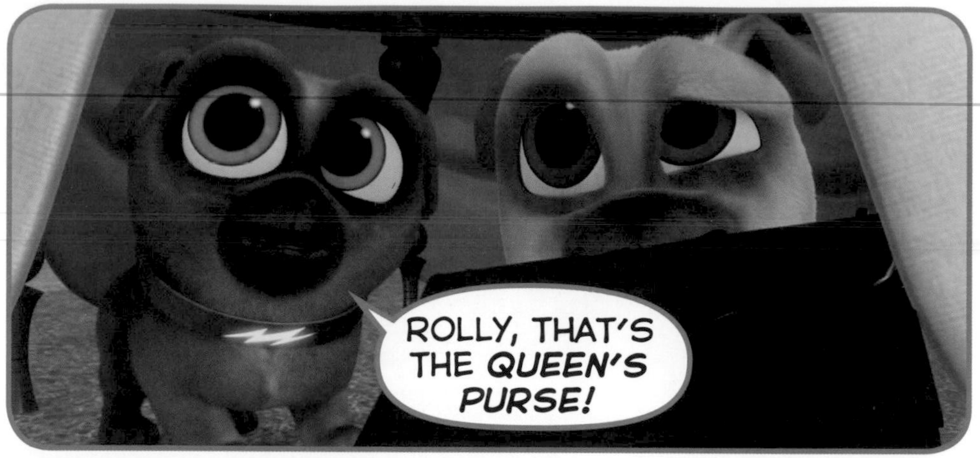
ROLLY, THAT'S THE *QUEEN'S PURSE!*

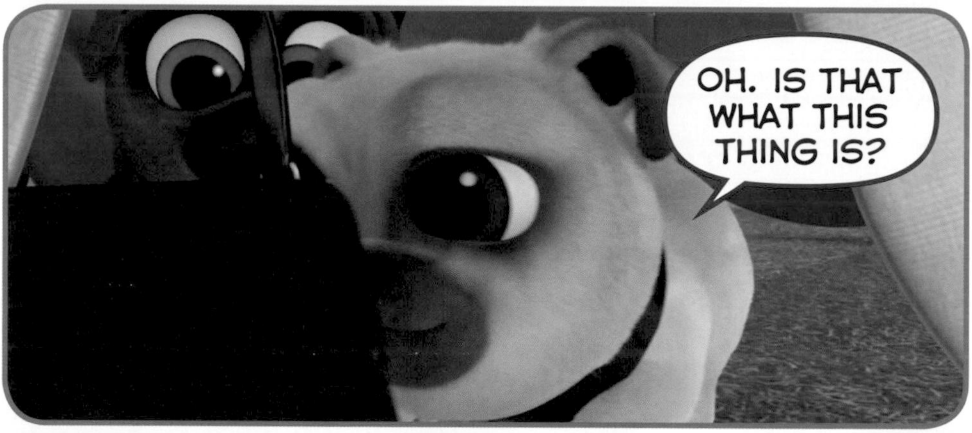
OH. IS THAT WHAT THIS THING IS?

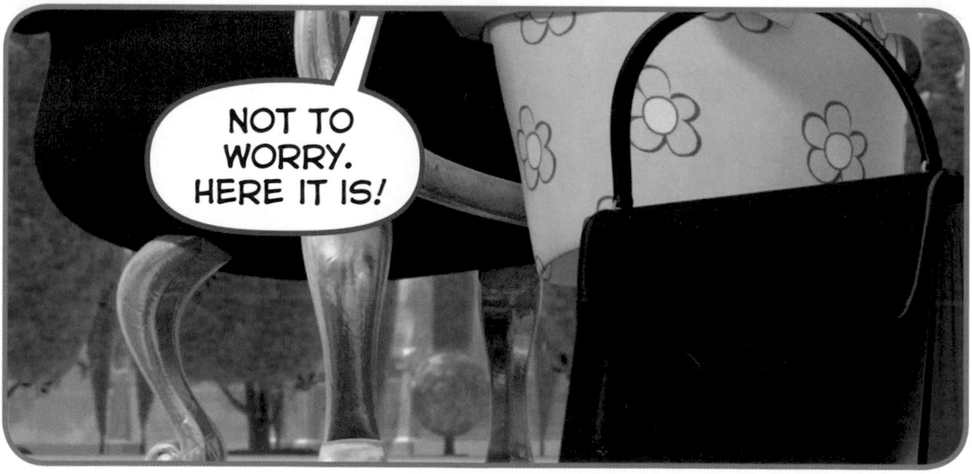
NOT TO WORRY. HERE IT IS!

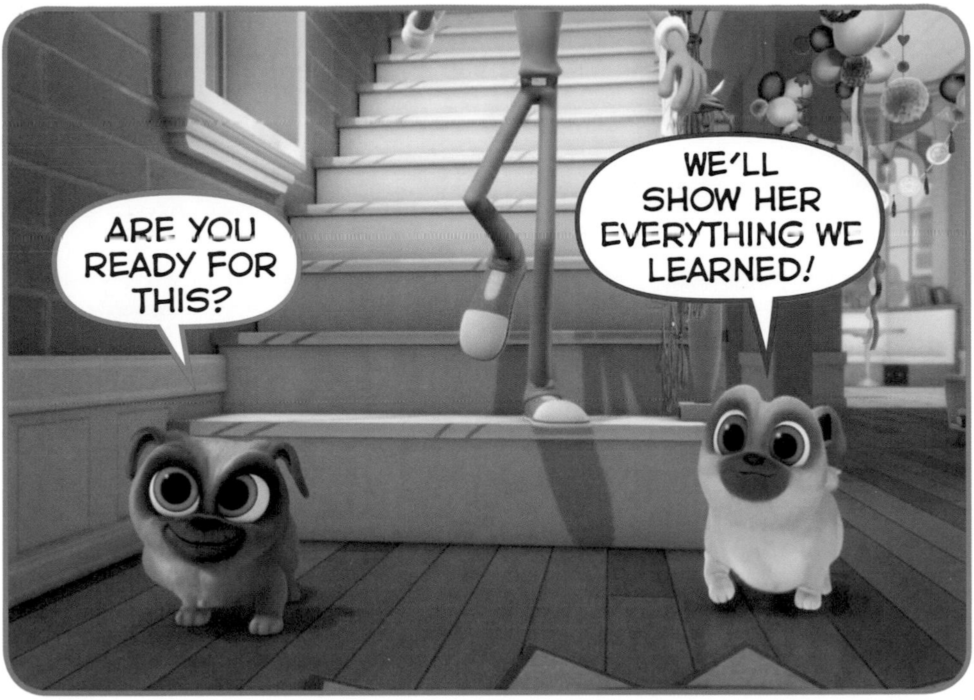
ARE YOU READY FOR THIS?
WE'LL SHOW HER EVERYTHING WE LEARNED!

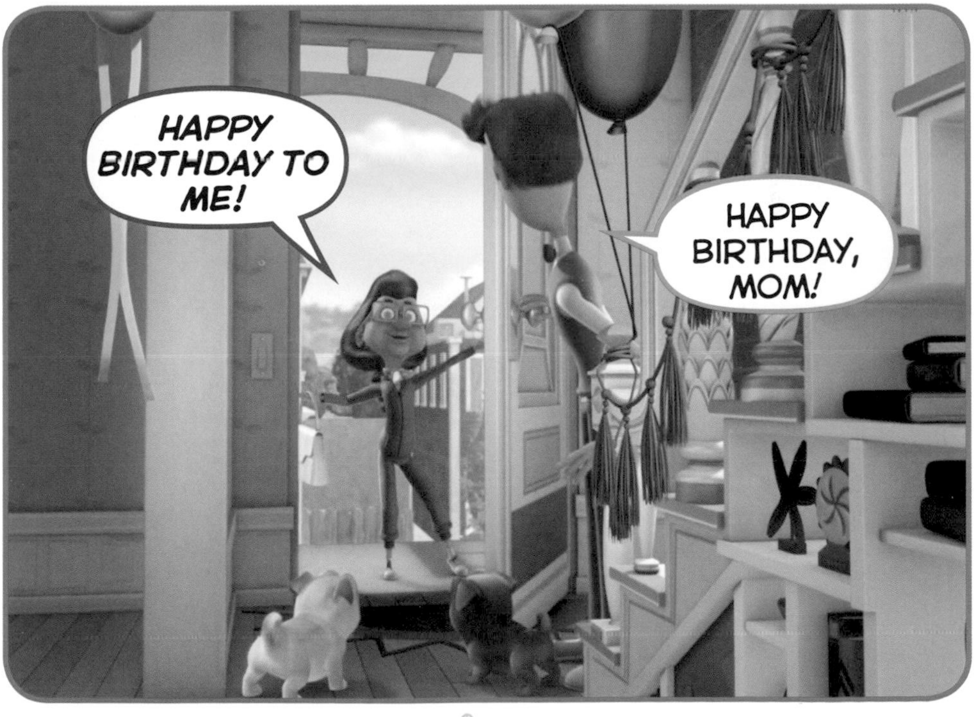
HAPPY BIRTHDAY TO ME!
HAPPY BIRTHDAY, MOM!

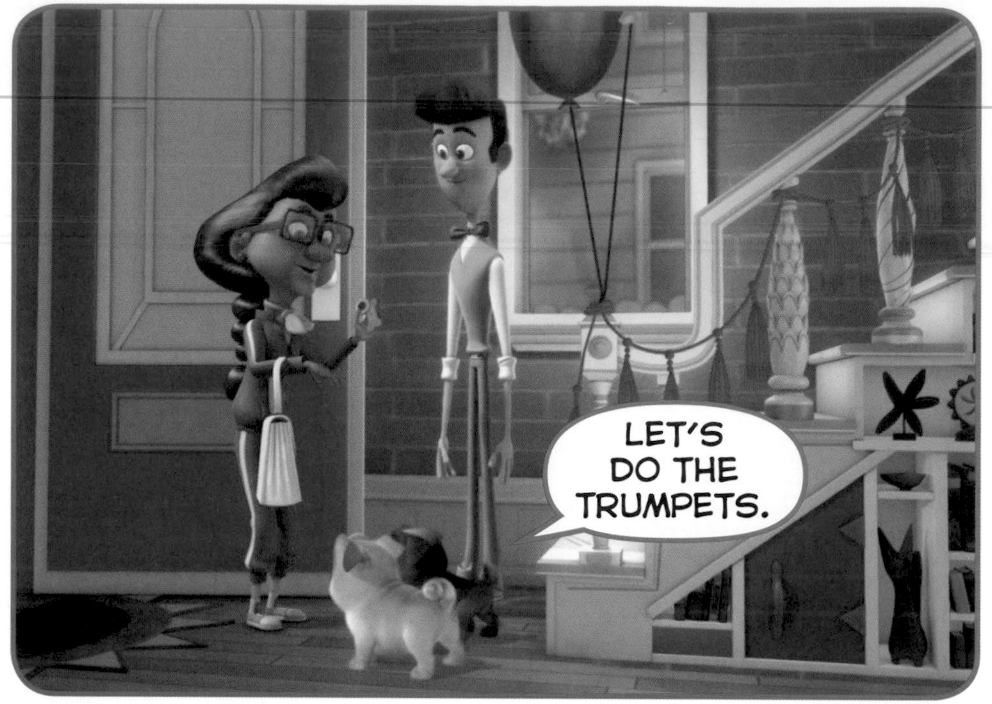
LET'S DO THE TRUMPETS.

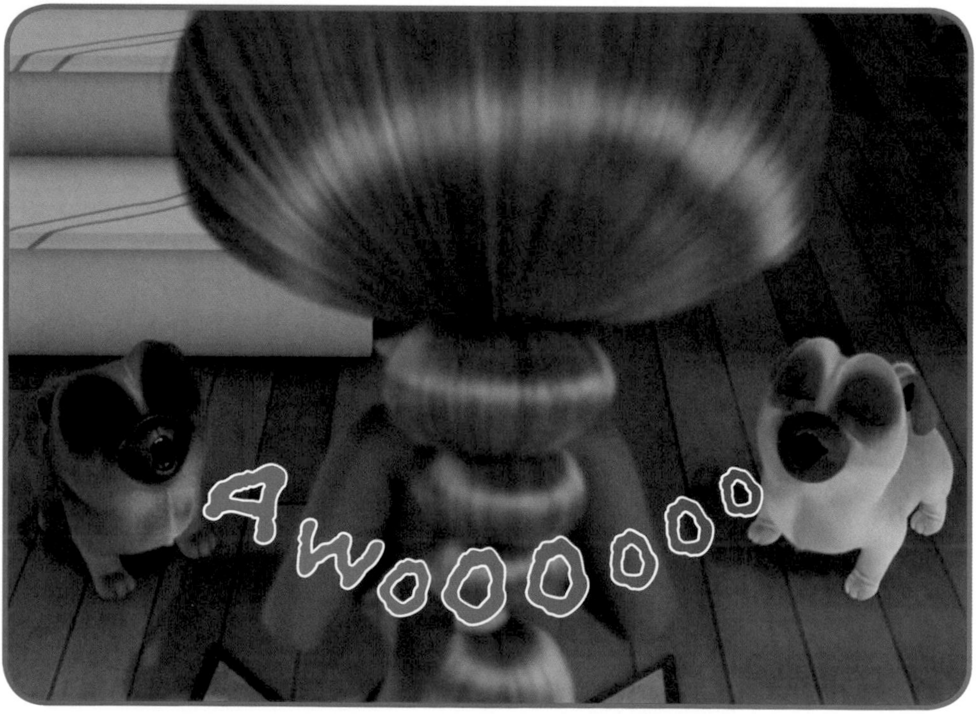
AWOOOOOO

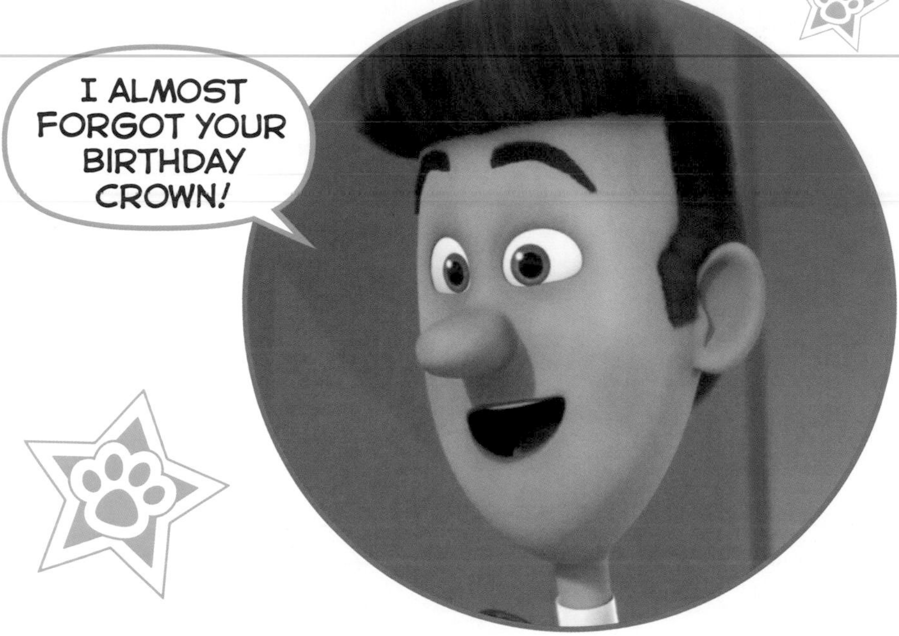
I ALMOST FORGOT YOUR BIRTHDAY CROWN!

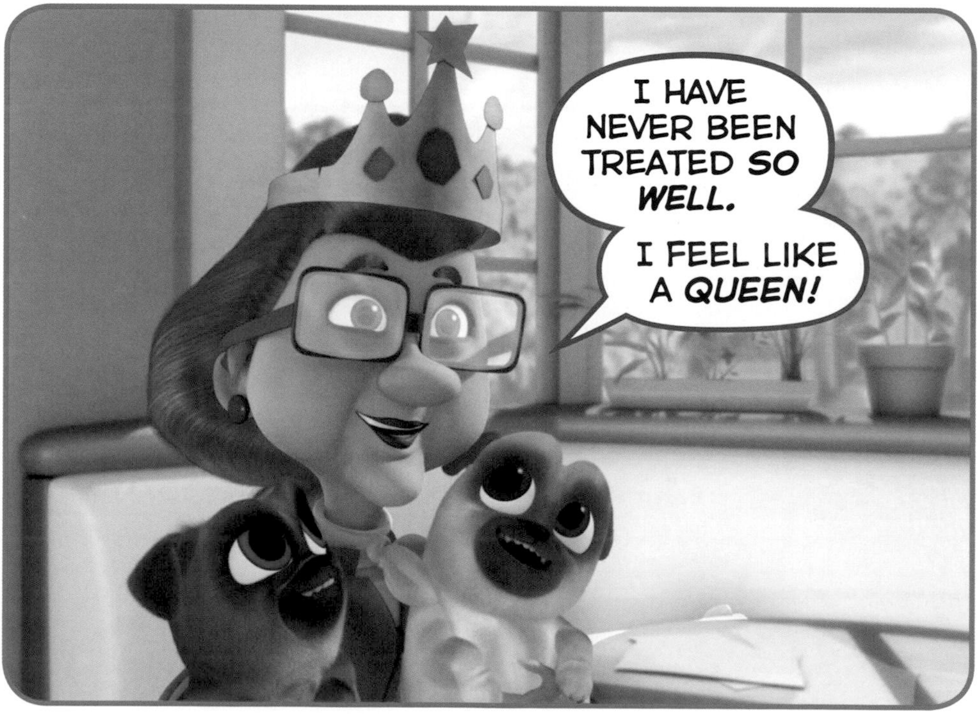
I HAVE NEVER BEEN TREATED SO WELL.
I FEEL LIKE A QUEEN!

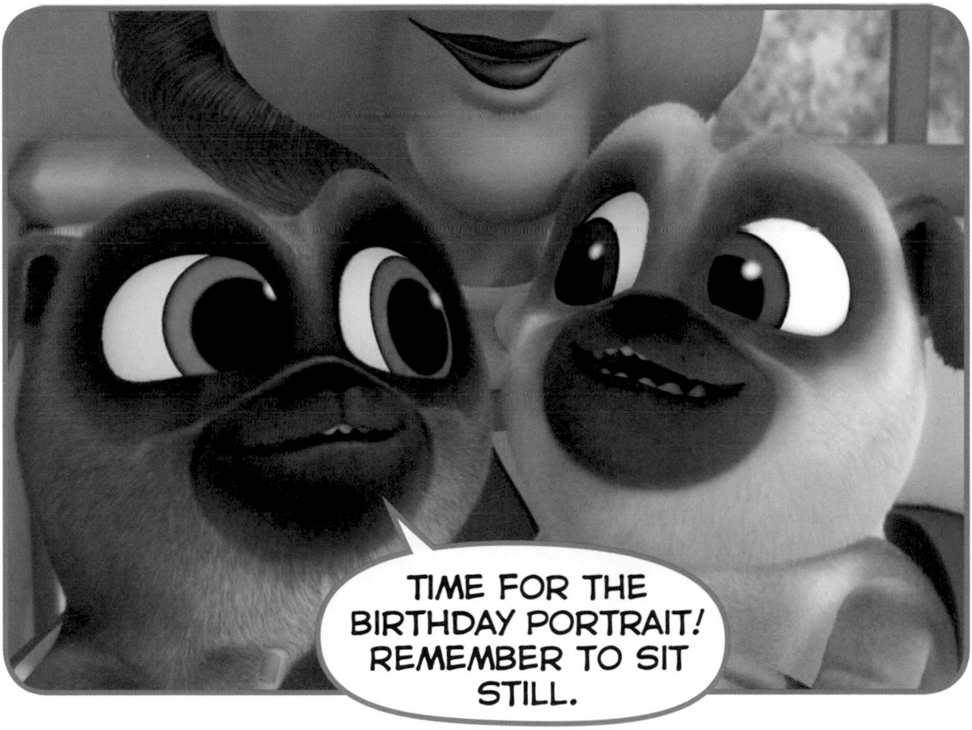
TIME FOR THE BIRTHDAY PORTRAIT! REMEMBER TO SIT STILL.

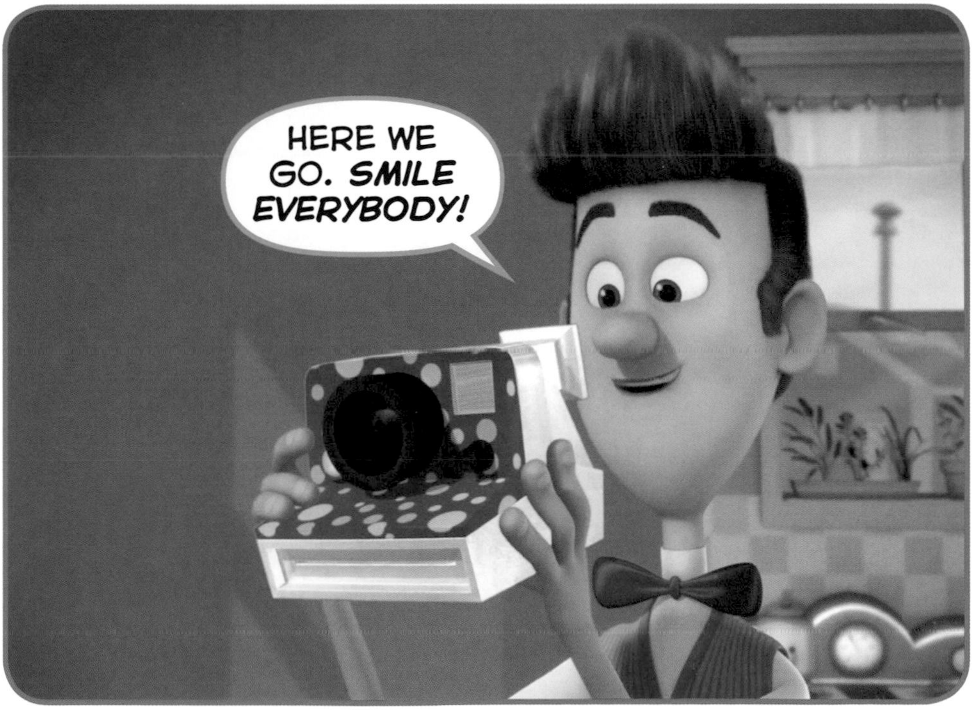
HERE WE GO. *SMILE EVERYBODY!*

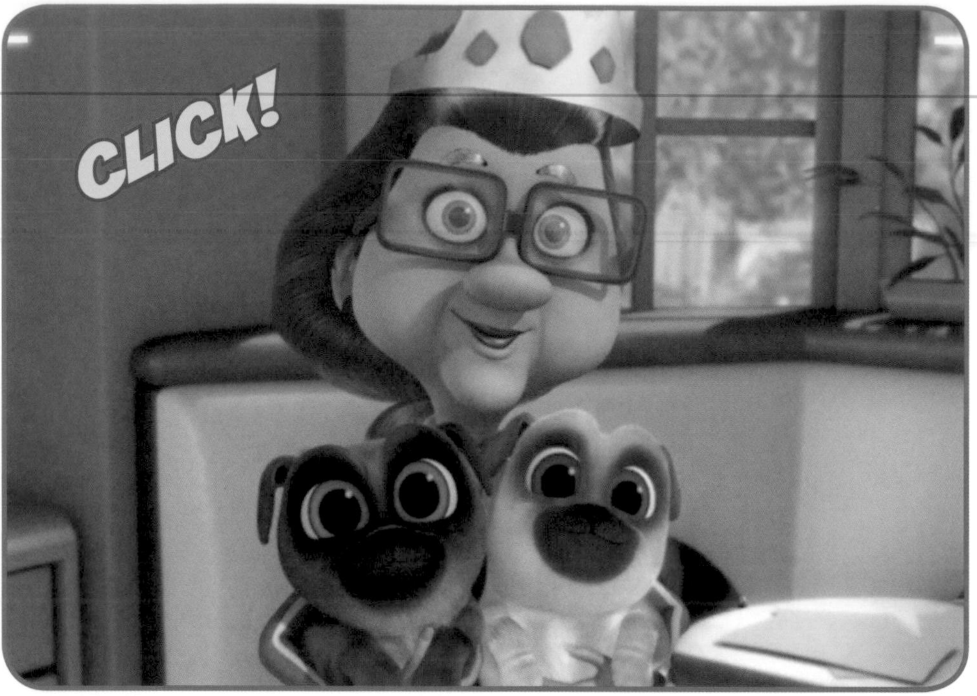
CLICK!

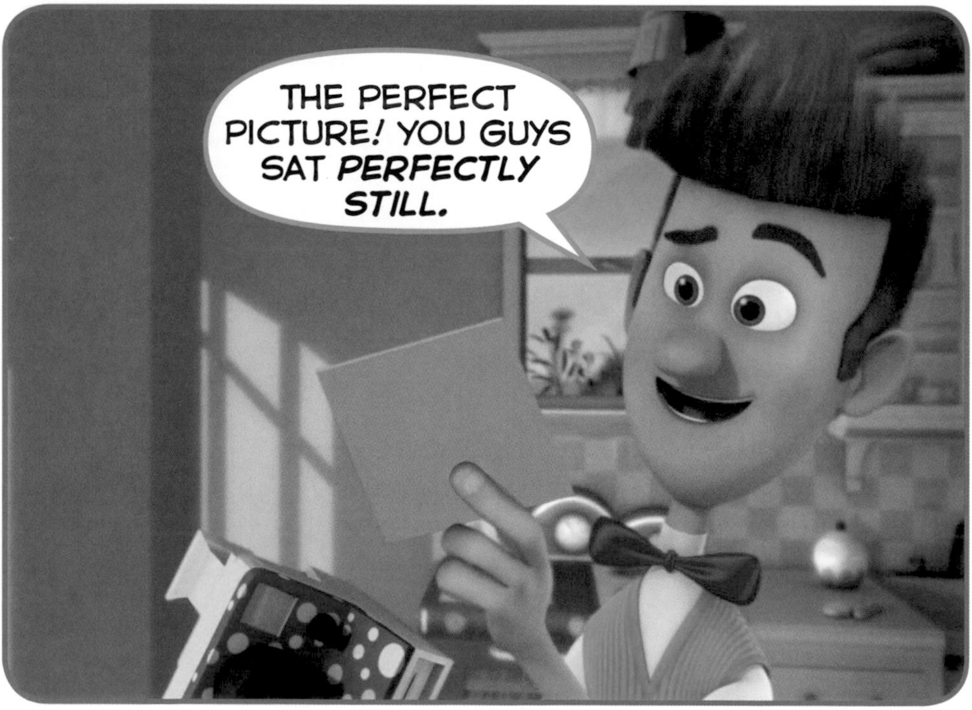
THE PERFECT PICTURE! YOU GUYS SAT *PERFECTLY STILL.*

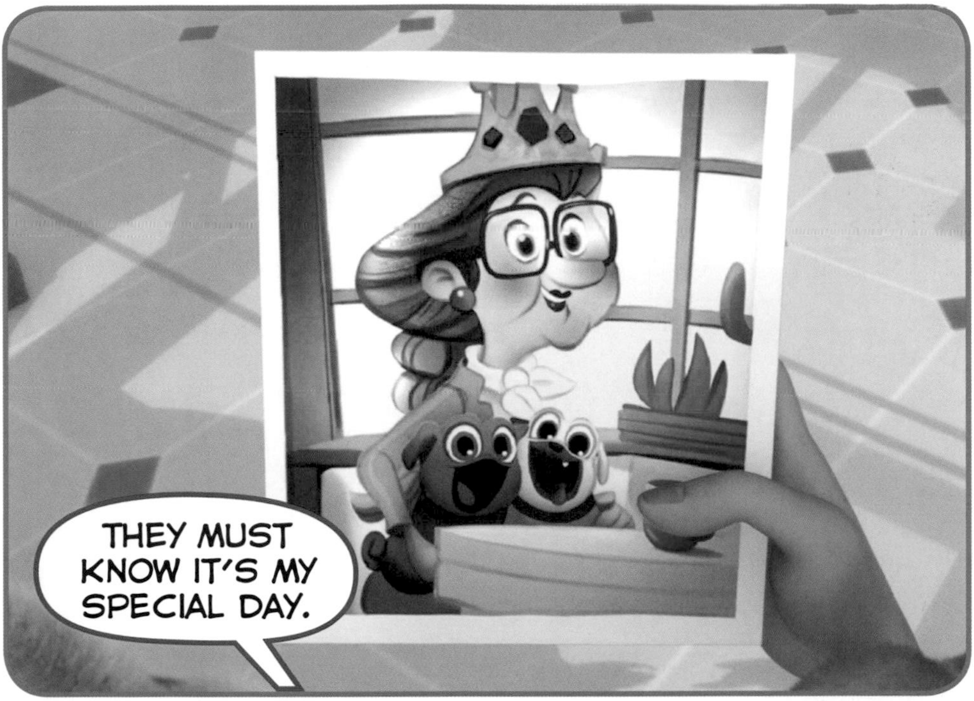
THEY MUST KNOW IT'S MY SPECIAL DAY.

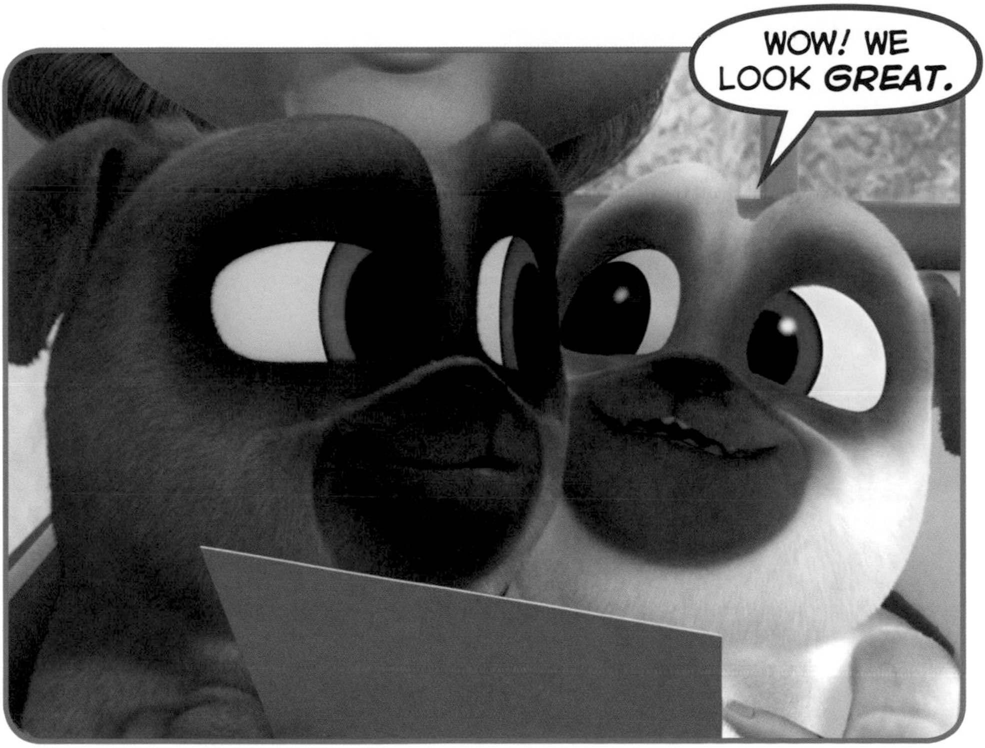
WOW! WE LOOK **GREAT.**

"Their Royal Pug-ness"

Created by
Harland Williams

Directed by
Stephanie Arnett

Supervising Directors
Trevor Wall
Don MacKinnon

Executive Producers
Sean Coyle
Richard Marlis
Carmen Italia

Written by
Bob Smiley

Storyboard by
Otis Brayboy

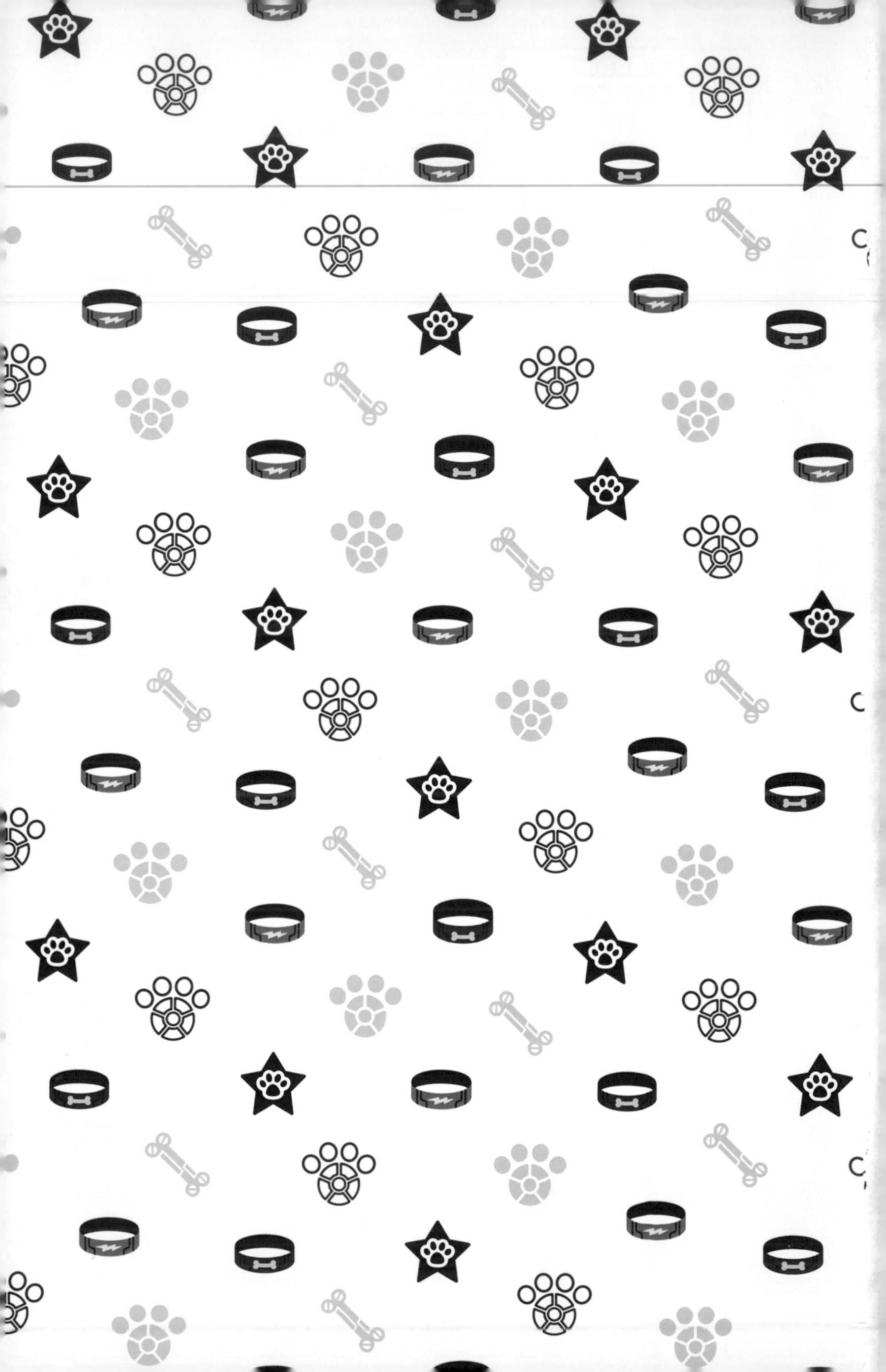